FOUR

Billy McLaughlin

E: billymclaughlinbooks@gmail.com
F: facebook.com/billymclaughlinbooks
T: twitter.com/bilbob20

Available:
Invisible
Lost Girl
In the Wake of Death
The Dead of Winter
The Daughter
Krampus
Fractured
Four

Download: Author.to/bmb

It's been an exciting time as I come to the end of writing 'Four'. This book was always intended to be a DI Phil Morris entry but started its life much earlier, scheduled between 'Lost Girl' and 'In the Wake of Death'. It's original title 'The Way the Rain Falls,' has been abandoned in favour of this new much swifter title, which is the essence of the book as it has gained and lost a few pounds in the three years that it has taken to finalise.

I want to thank everyone for their patience. Phil has been on a hiatus for almost two years. It is with pleasure that I once again hand him over to you and I hope that you enjoy where the characters have gone and where the stories have now taken them. This is my first dabble into the serial killer world and I have a lot to live up to. I just hope that the months of research and the endless questions will lead to a satisfying and engaging read.

I just want to lastly thank everyone for continuing to enjoy my work. I hope you'll continue to do so, and I look forward to hearing your feedback.

xxBilly

PROLOGUE

He has chosen the coldest night of the winter to dump his second victim. The most isolated, yet most open spot in the heart of the park. The rain will fall and lash her skin. The wind will scream in terror while she weeps. The cold will nip until she bleeds into defeat. She's been the gamer of the two conquests, yet his win will be just as inevitable as the first.

He smiles through the grid and watches her feel her way round the narrow space. She hasn't accepted her fate yet, which only makes him enjoy it more. Soon she will become like the first one, so tired from the scorn of nature that she will welcome her looming death. All he has to do is wait.

He grips his hand round the rusty tap of the old hose and twists it. It groans and shudders as it trickles to life. A poor murky substitute for the wrath of the rain.

The skies will split open and the rain will fall again. He is certain of it. It always does. For now, a flowing stream of brown liquid drops from the neck of the hose and splashes onto the girl's face. He watches her turn away and howl, falling into the mire of sodden dirt with a plop that echoes up into the air. He can't quite see her eyes, but he imagines them inflamed and burning up the twenty feet in plea of his mercy.

He wants to speak to her. To tell her why. Will it matter if she knows? To say it aloud, and someone hear it would be as satisfying as her death itself. Who will she tell after she is dead?

He grips the iron grid at the top of the shaft in his gloved hand and feels a surge of rage. Below him, the woman is nothing more than a writhing silhouette gasping against the relentless chill. Any minute now she will let out one more terrified gasp. Then it will be over. His work will be done here.

Two down! Two to go!

1.
21st January, 2019

Detective Inspector Phil Morris tightened the knot in his tie and brushed the flakes of rain from his shoulders. As he lowered himself briskly into the driving seat, he waited for his fiancé to take her place beside him. He shook the wet from his hair and groaned at the silver strands that were now growing round his ears. Nothing like a reflection to remind a person of their age.

'Sorry to keep you waiting,' apologised Kate, as she rushed into the car and slammed the door. 'There's always one more thing you forget to do.'

'First day nerves?' Phil asked, revving the engine and switching on the radio.

Kate Mulgrew, twenty years his junior had been up since long before dawn, brushing over her sallow complexion with just enough bronzer that she didn't look half dead. 'You can read me like a book. I'm so nervous. I don't know how many times I wanted to climb back under the duvet this morning and cancel the whole thing.'

'What stopped you?' Phil pulled out of the parking space, slipping into the oncoming traffic. As he sped towards the nearest slip road of the M74, he fired through the raging blizzard with little concern for the wet slushy roads.

Kate shrugged. 'I can't hide under the duvet every time I get nervous. I really want this degree. I want to have a future,' she paused. 'What kind of example would I be setting for Harry if I just quit anyway?'

'You don't have to worry about your future. I'll always take care of you,' said Phil. Once he'd changed into fourth gear and found his place in the middle lane, he rested his hand on her knee and gave it a gentle rub. 'I know you really want to succeed though, so just remember you're only there for a few weeks and then it's all written work for the rest of the year.'

She reached into the cotton bag and pulled a ring binder onto her lap, pushing his hand away in the process. 'I don't know whether that's a good or bad thing. I think most of my nerves are coming out of not knowing what I'll find there. What if I can't do anything to help? What if it's all just a wreck and I say something to make it worse.'

Phil smirked. 'It's a four-week placement Kate. Don't be too hard on yourself if you haven't saved the world in that time.'

She turned to him and gave him a gentle nudge on the arm. 'I know that. That doesn't mean I can't at least try to help.'

His mobile phone rang.

Donna Barclay's voice boomed loudly through the Bluetooth speaker. 'Phil, I'm at Jordanhill Park. Groundskeeper phoned in a dead body just after six this morning.'

'Jesus Christ,' he roared. 'Accidental?'

'Definitely not,' replied Donna. 'Similar to Michelle Evans. Obviously, we don't know the full details yet, but she was dumped down a pit and left to die.'

'Which part of the park? I'm dropping Kate off. It's her first day at Marina Cullen House.'

'Tell her good luck. Phil, will you be long. It's quite exposed here and we're not really getting any reprieve from this rain.'

'Thanks,' Kate said, cutting into their interaction.

For a moment, Phil detected a tone of irritation in Donna's voice. It was going to be one of those days.

'I'll be there in fifteen minutes Donna. The refuge is just off Byres Road.' He hit the end button, cutting Donna off mid-sentence.

Kate snickered. 'She sounds happy.'

He checked his reflection in the mirror once more. 'I don't know what's going on with her. She's been in a foul mood for weeks. Every time Steve comes into a room, she scowls like a rabid dog and bites his head off the minute he looks in her direction. It's ridiculous. She's becoming a right pain in the arse.'

'What's gotten up her nose?'

Phil shrugged again. 'I'd love to know.'

'She'll be fine. Wait until I ask her to be my bridesmaid. That should put a smile on her face.' Kate's voice trailed off as they pulled up to the front of an old tenement building halfway along Highburgh Road.

'And we're here,' he said anxiously. 'Good luck. I'll see you tonight.' Phil eyed the sign that waved beneath the refuge door; *Marina Cullen*, the woman who first founded the refuge back in nineteen-eighty-eight.

Kate moved slowly. She stretched her chin back awkwardly. 'I feel like my heart is going to jump out onto the pavement.' She leaned over and kissed him. 'Don't forgot I'll be late tonight. I've got a meeting with my mentor.'

Phil did his best not to rush her, though he knew time was not on his side now that a second body had turned up. 'You'll be fine. Steve wouldn't have suggested it otherwise. Steve swears by the manageress, said she's a right character but a heart of gold. Anyway, do you want me to pick you up after your meeting?'

Kate smiled knowingly. 'I'll be okay getting the bus. Anyway, I'll probably be home before you.' The car door flew open, bouncing in the wind as she laughed and threw her legs to the side. 'We should get Donna and Steve over for dinner. Maybe a few vinos will be enough to settle whatever is going on there.'

Phil held his hand up. 'If you want World War four on your hands, feel free. Tell me the time and date so I can be elsewhere.'

'Love you,' she whispered, delivering a sly wink as she got out of the car.

He waited a moment and watched her disappear into the building. He watched her turn one more time, just as he suspected she would, and gave her the biggest smile of encouragement he could muster. When she disappeared, he allowed himself to fall into the foggy wave of despair. Then he prepared himself for the sight of another dead body.

2.

The blizzard had thickened along the edge of Jordanhill Park, the sparse daylight curving round the clouds, the naked trees stretching in preparation of what was yet to come.

As Phil drove along the dirt road on the perimeter, his brake shuddered with every tiny clip he went over. In his mind's eye, he re-visited the image of Michelle Evans; her bare flesh battered, her eyes ablaze with inflammation, the horror expression on her face as she was slowly starved of breath. Most horrifying to him though was the posthumous branding to her forehead. A star, probably delivered by a branding iron once used on cows, had been left in a suspected bid to mark a killer's territory. No matter how many times he tried to bury the image, it just kept re-surfacing. Now, he was about to relive it in the broad light of day. Those people in regular jobs always thought he should be hardened to the snuffing of life. He wasn't.

Large iron gates lay wide open behind him, an inviting contrast to something playing out deep in the heart of the grounds. It was another half a mile to the last of the seven pit shafts in the area. Long since disused, it didn't take much to imagine they'd be the perfect place to hide a body, dead or alive. Phil pulled the car into a parking space longing for the frivolity of honeymoon dreams. He'd possibly shown Kate fifty brochures by now, but she was hell bent on only one place. Who was he to deny her it? Another thought that he disappeared quickly because he didn't want the first day of married life to be brushed with the terrible vision that awaited him today. No groom should walk down the aisle with thoughts of dead strangers.

He bypassed the uniformed figure tasked with documenting the arrival and departure of anyone stepping into the crime scene. A more boring task Phil could not imagine, yet the young man delivered it with the swagger of a fairground attendant.

Phil noted the people huddling on the nearby bridge who squashed into each other because, despite the fury of the winter, they were determined to witness every painfully slow event to unfold. If only they'd seen as many crime scenes as Phil had. He doubted they'd stand in minus six degrees for quite so long. Carnage always brought company. Today would be no different.

He scribbled half his signature, acquired a pair of gloves and headed into the hub. He knew most of their faces, though mulled over their names because there was nothing more embarrassing than admitting he didn't know someone's name when he'd met them seventy times.

The pit was a-flood with lights, each one raised and directed into the heart of the pit whilst a team of forensics poured painstakingly over every inch surrounding the dead woman's body. Round the edge of the pit was a wire grid and a rusty old tap that was dripping brown water. It looked like part of a larger contraption that might have covered the entire grid until it was broken off.

'Kate get to the refuge alright?' Steve Carter sidled up to Phil, seemingly unmoved by what was unfolding.

Phil rubbed his hands together to ward off the cold and nodded. 'I didn't know you were here.'

Steve lifted his eyes from the grizzly scene and for a moment it appeared that he had been wounded by Phil's deathly dry tone. 'The chief wants me as involved as possible. He thinks the best way of learning is to be in amongst the action. You don't mind, do you?'

'No', Phil replied, briefly turning to see that a conversation was taking place between Donna Barclay and Carrie Marshall. 'As long as you don't wind her up.'

Steve, a sturdy handsome thirty-year-old with a slick of curls and thick black brows to frame his crooked smile, shrugged. 'My breathing winds her up.'

'True!'

As if by telekinetic invite, Donna came storming towards them, face narrowed into an expression of rage. 'Did he tell you what he did?'

Here we go again, thought Phil. 'What?'

'Not here five minutes and managed to get his grubby paws all over the edge of the grid. He has probably contaminated it in a thousand different ways.'

'Calm down,' said Phil, mirroring her anger internally but knowing it wasn't the solution to a problem already spent. He spoke in stage whispers, holding his hands out to hush her. 'We can eliminate his prints very easily. It shouldn't be too hard to sort it out. The last thing I need is you cracking up.'

Donna turned to Steve and hissed. 'Why have you not got any gloves on? This could have been avoided if you'd followed the rules.'

Phil moved round her, taking lead over the situation. 'She's bloody right though. You should have been more careful. If we find prints or anything at this scene and they've been contaminated with yours, we'll have a job getting a warrant, let alone a conviction.'

Steve pulled his jaw back, half smiling and half grimacing.

Donna sighed loudly, apparently not appeased by the ticking off. 'Next time we'll have him abseil down the side of the pit with his mucky trainers on, piss round the edges and have an afternoon nap down there. May as well go the full shebang.'

Phil scolded her with an expression. He wasn't in the mood for her petulance today, yet he understood her frustration. He knew she hated Steve. It had been apparent ten minutes after he was placed with them and today, Steve had given her half a dozen more reasons to be infuriated by his presence. Whether she was right or wrong though, Phil was tired of distracting them, keeping them apart like two warring siblings.

'I'm going to speak to Carrie. Try and stay out of her way, Steve.' He thumbed towards Donna who stood with her back to them.

'Morning. This is getting to be a habit,' said Carrie, smiling through gritted teeth as she pulled her protective white overall tighter. 'I guess you already know about your boy wonder there?'

Phil tusked as he followed her towards the pit. 'Yes! Bloody idiot.'

Carrie cleared her throat and waved her hand away. 'Lesson learned; I hope. Although I don't know if he should be here if he's not up to speed on basic protocol.'

'He's excitable. New to our team and the chief wants to break him in the hard way. If he's got one thing on his side, it's his willingness to learn.' Phil grudged defending someone who had been so ham fisted with something as delicate as a murder scene, but he also believed that a senior should always publicly support his staff. He would rip Steve apart later. 'I'm sure we can make use of him.'

She shrugged and pointed through a square in the grid. 'It's your funeral.'

Phil could see the woman's frozen features, the burned sockets of her terrified eyes glaring up and the stalled inflammation of the star that had been branded on her forehead post-death. Her mouth stretched back revealing the pain she must have endured as she took her last breath. She wore little fabric, certainly not clothing anybody would have worn in this weather. 'I don't even need to ask if there are similarities. It's the same as Michelle Evans' death.'

Carrie nodded. 'Except, I would say at first glance, she died quicker. Hypothermia can set in very quickly if someone is exposed to these cold temperatures. Also, the groundskeeper checked the park on Friday before clocking off for the weekend and claims there was no-one here.'

'Either it means she died in less than seventy-two hours or that she was moved here near the end of her ordeal. How long until you have a time of death?'

'It wouldn't even take seventy-two hours for her to die. I'd say hours, less than a day even.'

'At least it would have been quicker than the first girl.'

'I wouldn't say that. Have you ever stood in a freezing cold wind with no clothes on for ten minutes? It would probably feel like hours. Imagine an hour down there with nothing on, with the wind and rain battering down on you. Multiply that dozens of times.'

'Any sign of sexual assault?'

'I know there was nothing on Michelle Evans. I

can't say for certain until we've carried out a proper post-mortem, but sexual intercourse doesn't seem to be the motivation here. We don't even know if the killer is a man.'

Donna joined them at that moment and bowed over the side of the pit. 'It's a man. No woman would do this to another woman. Murder is one thing. This is torture and humiliation.'

Carrie nodded her agreement. 'On a psychological level, he's deriving pleasure from torturing them. He already knows they're going to die. They don't know it. They will spend their last minutes hoping and praying that someone is coming for them. It's almost more sadistic than just stabbing them to death or strangling them.'

Donna sighed. 'I can't imagine how frightened they must be.'

Phil shook his head and grimaced. 'We need to get an identity as quickly as possible. We also need to find out what they have in common, employment history, relationships, friendships, where they socialise. I want a complete workover of their lives so we can start to piece together their final days. Once we make a connection, and I think we will, we can start to look for our killer. In the meantime, we need to be frugal with the details. I do not want that lot,' he cocked his head to the gathering media, 'getting wind of any of this. The last thing we need is a feeding frenzy by the media, or hysterical citizens losing it. We've got enough to deal with.'

'We can't keep it from the public forever,' insisted Donna. 'Especially if it does turn out to be a serial killer. People have a right to protect themselves.'

'Just as these young women have a right to

justice. Do you think we can do the best job for them if we're chasing after terrified callers who don't even know they've got anything to fear yet?' He looked towards the bridge and drew his eyes across the concerned faces, imagining the face of a killer among the waiting victims of a slaughterhouse. 'For now, we tell them what they need to know.'

3.

Kate had been sitting for forty-five minutes before someone noticed she was still waiting.

'I'm so sorry, has Natasha not come out to see you yet?' A muscly blonde woman, probably three or four years her junior, joined Kate in the musty hallway and sat on an orange seat to her left. 'She must have got caught up. It's always a little crazy in here on a Monday.'

Kate eyed the stone arch that curved above her head and surmised the building must have been a convent or something like it. The décor, or lack thereof reminded her of a trip she had once taken to a nunnery. Except there were no images of Jesus and no golden crucifixes. Just bare walls that were long overdue a lick of paint and the haunting echo of the fallen who too often walked inside them. She rather imagined it to be a place where everyone felt abandoned by God. What possible need could they have for a crucifix or the face of Jesus? 'It's no problem,' she answered politely, nervously pushing the tip of her thumbs together. 'I was probably too early.'

'Nothing wrong with being early,' said the blonde, her thick Aberdonian accent bouncing along the empty corridor. 'I'm Charlie by the way. I'm one of the support staff here.'

'Kate,' she replied, her nerves forming a croak in her throat. 'How long have you worked here?'

'Two years, give or take. I was a volunteer when I first moved to Glasgow and now, I'm in with the bricks.' She shifted quickly in her seat and looked flatly at Kate. 'Have you done any work like this before?'

Kate hated when someone focused on her. Even as a child, she preferred to drift into the background, playing quietly in a corner and slipping off early from places so no-one would see her come or go. She now suspected her mother's extreme and sometimes volatile behaviour was responsible. 'No,' she finally offered, hoping the short sharp answer would be enough to deflect attention back to Charlie.

'Okay,' said Charlie, winking. 'Don't worry, everyone's really nice. I know its daunting when it's your first day. They only bite if you use the last of the milk and don't replace it. Which reminds me, the way to Natasha's heart is cream buns and coffee. Get that right, and she won't be letting you go in four weeks.'

'I'll keep it in mind,' said Kate, letting her shoulders fall. She hadn't realised just how rigidly she'd been holding herself until she noticed the ache in her upper back.

'Kate?' A woman arrived at the end of the corridor, her heels scraping against the stone-cold floor tiles.

'Hi,' answered Kate, flinching at the sudden arrival.

'I'm so sorry,' said the woman, stretching out a bejewelled hand to greet Kate. 'It's been like a carnival this morning. I honestly didn't forget you were coming.' The woman laughed riotously; the inside of her silver ring cold against Kate's palm. Natasha was older than she sounded on the telephone, a grey quiff on her slender face and a checked suit that rested against her wine glass figure. 'I'm Natasha, if you haven't guessed. Can I get you anything?'

Kate recounted the earlier conversation with Charlie, smiled and sidled up to her new boss. 'Can I have a coffee?'

It must have been the magic words. 'Abso-bloody-lutely,' boomed Natasha. 'A woman after my own heart. I'll show you the kitchen and tell you a little about the service and what we do here.'

Kate swung her bag over her shoulder and followed Natasha to the kitchen. She watched as Natasha clattered around a cupboard for some clean mugs. 'If you're not quick in here, you'll likely die of dehydration.' She pushed the button down on the kettle before turning to face Kate. 'So, tell me a bit about yourself. Steven said you're married to his boss.'

'Not yet,' said Kate, rubbing her finger excitedly on her own, rather modest engagement ring. 'We're setting a date soon.'

'How lovely,' shrilled Natasha. 'I remember the excitement well. I've been married twenty-two years and I'm still in love with the bugger.'

Kate wanted to say something nice, maybe comment that Natasha didn't look old enough to be married nearly quarter of a century. Was it rude to tell a white lie to be polite? Perhaps she could ask the secret to longevity. 'Do you need any help?'

'No, that kettle takes its own sweet time. I hope you're not too thirsty. If it's not missing or broken crockery, it's a kettle that's work shy.'

Kate laughed. 'That sounds like every appliance we own.'

'Get used to it. No matter how slow the microwave, the kettle or the toaster goes in the house, my husband always goes slower.'

Another laugh, heartier this time. 'To be fair, Phil has told me to replace what I want. He's had most of our stuff since long before we met. I've always believed I shouldn't spend money I didn't earn.'

'Admirable, but foolish,' said Natasha with a mocking pout. 'What's his is yours. The first rule of marriage. My husband has handed me every penny since the day he put this on my finger.' She wiggled her wedding finger, the diamond dazzling against the hanging light. 'His father is just the same.'

Kate didn't want to have to explain that Phil would be her second husband. She'd been married once before but hadn't enjoyed the conventions of married life. The marriage had ended so violently that it had taken her this past three years to learn to trust again. Perhaps it was the reason she was so nervous now.

Natasha broke the silence when she slammed a mug of coffee on the table. 'I prefer to bring my own coffee in. I didn't have time this morning so we're settling for this instant garbage.'

Kate didn't mind the instant stuff. She'd had worse. She hadn't always lived in the luxury that Phil afforded her. She simply smiled though. Natasha and Charlie had been so lovely to her that she dare not mention anything of her past. How could she tell them she had once lived on the street and that a kind detective had rescued her from the clutches of a maniac? Perhaps it was entirely fitting that she should do her work placement here. Or perhaps it was just a little too close to home.

As she framed her thoughts and blew into the steaming mug, Kate realised she had always feared rejection. Not just rejection, but judgement. The logic in her told her she had nothing to fear because she couldn't tell them anything about her life that they didn't see every day. There was still that niggling doubt. It wasn't a chance she was prepared to take.

4.

Phil paced the incident room floor with growing anger. He dragged his stare away from the face of Michelle Evans, no longer able to contain his disgust. They had a second body, none of them in any doubt that their young woman had fallen prey to the same sadistic killer as the first victim.

It was certainly novel; a killer who barely laid a finger on his victims. This was one who did the catching, but not the gutting.

Donna, the lone female in a room full of men, ran her pen under her notes as she read aloud what she'd written. 'Victim number one, aged twenty-six, originally from Belfast and moved to Glasgow only three short years ago. Not much contact with her family, probably due to the geographical distance according to her mother and not a very large social circle.'

'Which makes her very easy to disappear,' interjected Phil.

'Post-mortem found she died of cardiac arrest when her body dipped below thirty-three. Melatonin injected into her neck, an acid spray on her eyes, designed to disarm her just long enough to carry her from the site of abduction to the place she'd be left to die. From the dirt in her nails and the scratches at the side of the pit, I'd hazard a guess that she probably fought as long as she could. She was dead within fourteen hours. A branding after death seems to be some sort of calling card, something that the killer probably relates to. No sign of sexual assault and no apparent human contact. CCTV footage gives us some insight into her final movements though the spot of abduction is a blind spot between Cathcart

Road and Victoria Road in the south side of Glasgow.'

Phil nodded in agreement. 'Twenty-six years old? We're attributing her death to heart attack? It all sounds so bloody natural yet there's nothing natural about it.' He eyed the photo of Michelle Evans, placed at the centre of the wall with a plethora of strings leading to a various assortment of clues that made no sense whatsoever.

Steve entered the room, his boyish face concealed by the steam from a mug of tea.

Donna's eyes rolled back in her head just long enough that Phil noticed her reaction. 'Don't worry, I didn't want one,' she muttered.

Steve spoke again, this time his face more serious. 'Did forensics find any fingerprints on the dead woman's body? Or a hair? Something that might allow us to identify her?'

'Nothing but an acid solution round her eyes, a pin prick at the vein of her neck and a brand to her forehead,' said Phil, already feeling slightly defeated. 'Human skin is porous. It's nigh on impossible to pick up on fingerprints or any human residue. In addition to that, Michelle's body took a rather severe beating from the weather. I doubt we'll be much luckier with our second victim.'

'There must be something that ties them together though.'

'It looks almost ritualistic,' said Phil, tapping a green inker on the bone of his wrist. 'All we're waiting for is confirmation that the acid spray and the sedative are the same and that'll be enough for us to link them both.'

Steve took a sip from his coffee and then cleared his throat. 'Any signs of sexual assault prior to death?'

Phil shook his head. 'No! Sex isn't the motivation here. It seems more about control and humiliation. I doubt they'll find anything on the second woman's body that wasn't found on Michelle.'

Donna continued to flick the pages of her notebook, continuously drawing her eyes across her own scribbles. She was clearly hoping that if she read it enough times it might reveal something they'd previously missed. 'Michelle was last seen at the pharmacy at the corner of Cathcart Road. That's three streets away from her flat. We can see her exit the shop on CCTV. It's once she turns onto Calder Street that she simply vanishes.'

'Nobody just vanishes though, do they? At that time of the evening those areas are usually quite busy. Surely someone would have seen a scuffle, don't you think?'

Phil looked at the picture of Michelle Evans that was taken on her birthday a few months before, her almond eyes staring out in sadness as if she knew it might be her last year on this planet. 'Which suggests she might have initially gone voluntarily.'

'Which means she might have known her captor,' interjected Steve. 'To get into someone's car, you have to know them and trust them.'

'So, there was a relationship. The thing that puzzles me though is the distance between their bodies being dumped. Michelle was dumped in a manhole in a secluded part of Linn Park and our second victim was dumped in Jordanhill Park. There's nearly thirteen miles between the two.'

'We don't know enough about the killer, or his motives, or the girls to know why they've been left in those locations. Perhaps it's simply random. Or maybe the locations mean something to the killer. Until we know who victim number two is, decipher the linkage between them both and find out what the killer does next, I don't think we'll learn anything by focusing on it.'

Donna was tapping her foot impatiently now and running her fingers across the notes. She sat a plastic cup of water precariously against another set of notes, little regard for balance and eyed the words on the page pensively. 'When I spoke to her mother, Mrs Evans was certain there were no men in Michelle's life. Perhaps she just didn't keep her mum in the loop. Daughters can be notoriously secretive. My mum thought my first boyfriend was my gay best friend for nearly nine months. I didn't bother to correct her.'

'Only you,' laughed Phil.

'Mrs Evans also said Michelle had no enemies. They live in different countries. I find it hard to believe that, one; a good-looking girl like her didn't have male interest and, two; that she got to twenty-six years old without making a single enemy. Maybe her mother doesn't want to face just how far from each other they'd become.'

'I don't think it's a reflection on how close they were. As you said, it's not unthinkable that a young woman would want to keep her more embarrassing secrets from her parents. I don't think we should confuse a geographical distance with an emotional distance,' advised Phil. 'She's not unlike most of the other parents we come across. Most think their child is a saint before you even throw into the mix that they've been tragically taken from them.'

Donna nodded agreeably.

'I also don't think we should assume she has

enemies,' said Steve, almost accusingly.

Phil fired him a warning shot; a look that was saying do not mess with her, you've already got her wound up enough.

Steve took the warning and slipped into a nearby seat.

'By all accounts, it seems her social activities were low key. To be fair, I don't know when she'd have found time to socialise,' said Phil. 'She worked a part time job in a bar, volunteered in various support services and was a full-time student. With a calendar that full, they'd have to invent an eighth day to fit in a life as well.'

'Then perhaps we speak to her boss. Bars are notorious places to acquire the attention of people with unhealthy fixations,' said Steve, as if he was taking from experience. 'Perhaps it was a colleague? Or someone who drank there?'

'Good idea, let's start to pick this haystack apart.'

Phil drew his eyes from the picture of the sad young woman who looked so lonely to the picture of her post-mortem and sighed. 'If I had just one body, I might have thought it was someone with an obsession with her. Or jealousy. It does look very personal. Now that we're dealing with a second body, I'm not so sure.' He thumbed his chin before tapping on the board. 'I just keep thinking that they must have known the killer.'

'You know, I've had the same feeling. If only pictures told stories,' said Donna, an eerie quality to her voice.

Phil stood. 'Maybe they do,' he whispered sadly, stepping closer to the board. 'Every dead body has a story to tell. We just don't know what Michelle's is yet.’

5.

The sound of a child screaming distracted Kate from the task of devouring her small tub of tuna salad. It was so piercing to her that she almost knocked the tub over with her fork. When the screaming didn't end, she rose from her seat and made her way towards the family room at the far end of the corner.

As she approached the door, the screaming becoming so vibrant she wanted to cup her ears closed with her hands, Kate could hear the pleading cries of the child's mother.

'Daniel,' said the woman, her voice quivering in desperation. 'Stop it right now. There's nobody there.'

When Kate finally reached the door, the taste of lemon drizzled tuna still on the roof of her mouth, she found the child thrashing on the floor whilst the young woman tried to pull him closer. 'Is everything okay?' She felt ridiculous for even asking because it was evident that nothing was okay at all.

The young woman merely widened her eyes and returned to the business of calming her son.

It was an image that might haunt Kate later because it seemed almost familiar to her. Once upon a time she'd had to comfort her traumatised son following a horrific event in her life. Thankfully, she'd never had to bring Harry to a place that might have accentuated his terror. Just one of a hundred reasons for her to love Phil. 'Daniel?' Kate entered the room, her hands held out so she could attempt to soothe the situation. 'My name's Kate. I'm just new here today.'

The screaming had subsided and dipped to a wheezing whimper.

‘Do you want to tell me what it is you saw?’ She hadn’t really known what had taken place but had deciphered the boy had been disturbed by something he had seen, something neither his mother nor her were privy to.

His breathing began to level.

‘You know, maybe we can look together. Would that be okay?’ Kate hoped the panic she felt rumble in her stomach was staying under the radar. The last thing she needed was to upset the little boy more.

His mother’s shoulders rose, and she let out a massive breath, a sigh of relief that sounded like it had been waiting in her chest forever and beyond.

Kate rubbed her shoulder. Again, she questioned herself because she didn’t know if she should show such tactility towards one of the residents. She wondered about her boundaries. Had she already crossed them? Where were the staff who managed the refuge? Surely someone else must have heard such a violent scream. ‘Come here sweetheart,’ she said, her voice barely more than a whisper.

Daniel stood, barely noticing his mother was now flattening the ruffle on the back of his shirt. ‘The bad man was here.’ He pointed towards the guarded window.

‘Really?’ Kate took his hand and led him just near enough that he could see on to the street. ‘Let me have a look.’ She shook her head. ‘See, nobody there.’

The boy looked disheartened, the tears now beginning to dry on his soft plump cheeks. ‘It’s different when nobody else is here.’ He sounded broken but determined of his truth, his eyes evidently haunted by whatever it was that had created the commotion in the first place.

Kate led him back to the red sofa in the corner of the room. 'Is he having nightmares?'

The mother rubbed her bleary eyes, a lifetime of exhaustion now pulling on her lids. 'Nightmares, day terrors, monsters under the bed, monsters in the street. You name it, he's having them. I've tried to speak to my doctor about it, but she says it's the trauma of what he's witnessed. Once he feels safe somewhere, it'll stop. That's the theory anyway.'

Kate nodded agreeably, unsure whether those scars really did heal but knowing that every day they became a little less deep.

'Sorry, are you new here?'

'Yes,' replied Kate, flushing. 'I didn't mean to burst in. I just heard the screams and thought there might be something wrong.'

'That's okay,' answered the boy's mother, her breathing beginning to settle. 'I can use all the help I can get. It might look like I'm coping better than him,' she nodded towards Daniel. '-but it only seems that way. I don't have the energy to scream. Nor do I want to have someone pat me on the shoulder and tell me everything's going to be alright.'

'The look of pity,' offered Kate. 'The little rubs on the back that feel like someone is telling you to calm down when there's no reason to be calm at all. I remember them all too well.'

The girl looked surprised. 'I'm Rochelle, by the way. I just moved in a couple of days ago. They say I'll be here for a week or two before they find me temporary housing. That's if they don't kick me out because of Daniel.'

'I'm sure they won't. Everybody who is here has probably experienced similar and probably have kids who are just as traumatised. I don't think you should worry too much about what other people are saying.' She paused. 'Sorry, I haven't even introduced myself. I'm Kate, one of the volunteers. This is a four-week placement as part of my degree.' She handed a block of Lego to Daniel who now seemed much calmer and content to assemble the highest building his arms would allow him to build. Kate would never have known it was the same child who had been hysterical a few minutes ago.

'I'm guessing you've had some similar experiences to the other women in here,' surmised Rochelle.

Kate simply nodded her head. She wasn't sure how much she could say, and she certainly didn't want to get on the wrong side of anyone on her first day.

'I can tell. You're not like the others. You don't have the look.'

'The look?' Kate's forehead dipped as lines formed above her eyebrows.

Rochelle shrugged. 'You know, when they look at us and wonder why we would allow ourselves to be abused. You see it all the time. They speak to you with the most sympathy they can muster, but they're secretly wondering why you would stand for someone punching you in the face. They don't think they would tolerate it. They only think that because it has never been a reality for them.'

'You and I both know that's not how it works.'

Rochelle snorted. 'They know it too.' She looked at the empty doorway with mild disgust, as if it were the entrance to a world that had done her too many wrongs. 'They think if they separate themselves from it, sit on the outside looking in, then it could never happen to them. They don't think their husbands, or their sons have the capacity to be monsters.'

'Not all men are monsters.'

'Not all women are victims.'

Kate turned back to the little boy, his sunken eyes beneath a gentle wave of dirty fair curls. He looked nothing like her Harry, yet she could almost imagine her own son in exactly that position. She had to shake her head to discard the image before it became burned in there forever.

'You know it didn't start out like that for me,' interrupted Rochelle, shattering the momentary silence.

Kate gasped lightly and eyed the room, the gaudy orange walls starting to play havoc with her eyes. 'No?'

'I met Pete when I was seventeen. We had the perfect life, at least in my mind. He worked hard, he loved kids and treated me like royalty. I thought life was going to be amazing for us. I had seen him angry, but never at me. Most of the time his anger would be verbal, ranting about someone at work, shouting abuse at other drivers, getting upset about the football results. He would always run out of steam eventually and I'd just put it down to him having to get it out of his system.'

'And did he?'

Rochelle looked pensive. 'Sometimes. More often than not.'

'When did it change?'

Rochelle leaned back, as if blocking Daniel out of her vision would also block him from hearing. 'When I had Daniel. It was little things at first. He'd get annoyed that I was too tired for sex. I never felt like a natural mum, so everything took its toll. I felt anxious. Pete would tell me to calm down. He seemed gentle about it at first. Then he seemed to get angrier and angrier. Until one night- '

'He hit you?'

Rochelle tightened her eyes, either to fight back the tears or conjure a long unwanted memory. She ran her index finger of her right hand along the lower rim of her eye. 'Christmas Eve, 2015. He was so drunk he barely managed a slap.'

'He still managed it though,' said Kate, her response dripping in disgust. She quickly berated herself for passing judgement. That wasn't what she was here to do.

'Months passed, it never happened again. I mentioned it once and he said it had been an accident. He was stressed and alcohol had taken over. He wasn't that type of man, he told me. I believed him.' Rochelle flinched, as if weary from her own stupidity. 'Then next time it was a shove. I fell over the table, split my head open and had to go to A&E. Only four stitches, not exactly a battle scar.' She rustled the paper hankie she'd apparently been hiding in her hand since Kate's arrival.

'I escaped without a scar,' said Kate, shocking herself with an impromptu admission. She wasn't even sure why she'd said it. As she ran her mind back through grains of time, she clutched her wrist and sighed. 'I was lucky because he'd never hit me before. Our life before that had been frustrating at best. I married him because he seemed safe. It transpired he had a raging psychosis and had been concealing it with medication and secret trips to psychiatry. I didn't even know the man I was married to.'

Rochelle cocked her head, frowning with obvious anticipation for whatever Kate was about to say next.

‘I’m sorry,’ she finally offered. ‘I shouldn’t have said that. I don’t know what made me say it.’

‘Hey, its fine. We’ve all got our story, right? You shouldn’t be afraid to be human.’

Kate felt a twinge of awkwardness, not full-blown guilt, but a knowledge she shouldn’t have gone there. It was completely unprofessional. The refuge wasn’t about her, or her past. It certainly wasn’t there to assist her in exorcising what was left of her demons.

Rochelle spoke again. ‘Hey, don’t be so hard on yourself. I’m guessing this is the first time you’ve been in a place like this. Me too. I know the other women in here will appreciate someone being on their side. No, not just on their side, but from a similar situation. It doesn’t feel like it sometimes, but we’re the lucky ones because we were strong enough to leave.’

Kate was about to apologise again when she heard a voice enter the room.

‘Can I have a word, Kate?’

She stood when she found Natasha standing in the doorway. ‘Sure,’ she said, her face flushing. How long had the woman been there? Had she heard the conversation between Kate and Rochelle? From the look on her face, Kate suspected she had. As she joined Natasha in the hall, already feeling the chill from the woman’s frosty demeanour, Kate knew exactly what she was about to be told.

‘Did your lecturer speak to you about the importance of confidentiality?’

Kate smiled. ‘Of course. It goes without saying.’

Natasha snorted slightly as she pursed her lips together. ‘Then, he would also have spoken to you about separating your private life from that of the people you're supporting.'

It was at that moment that Kate longed for a wall to fall between the two, some divider that would allow her not to hear the woman's scathe whilst also hiding her own beaconed face. 'Yes,' she finally managed to muster, the whisper of a scolded child.

'We don't just advise it for the safety of our residents, we advise it for your own protection as well. You're dealing with some very vulnerable people. Vulnerable people can be desperate, and you don't want to get on the wrong side of somebody who is desperate. You especially do not want them to know more about you than necessary.'

Kate nodded, standing just long enough for Natasha to give her a comforting shuffle of the arm. When she walked back to Rochelle, she found the young woman hovering near the door. Suddenly she understood exactly what Natasha had said to her. Perhaps she didn't want Rochelle knowing more about her than she needed to. She smiled awkwardly, wondering how much Rochelle had heard and then turned her focus to Danny. 'Hey, little fella. Let's see what else we can build with that Lego.'

6.

The killer approaches the mirror with a look of contempt on his face. His story is imprinted round the circles of his eyes, shreds of a past that he knows he can never escape. Sometimes he wishes he could be a ghost, or a vampire, or something that could shift from one place to the next unnoticed. He recalls a time where all he wanted was to be seen. Long before he wished to be invisible.

He recalls himself as he once was. A lanky boy shrouded in a mop of unkempt hair and bespectacled eyes. Before he traded for his new self.

He hears the newsreader blaring from the television, an inappropriately congenial delivery of a story he already knows. It makes him smile a little. The press furore hasn't quite kicked in but is already gathering momentum. A budding warning that hasn't quite penetrated yet.

He stares himself down, a steely glower at the man he barely recognises but has grown to admire. He switches the television off because Miss Congenial has handed over to a grey-haired male with an East Coast squawk and he's already starting to feel the strain of a migraine.

He looks at the photographs on the wall; four young women with their eyes scrubbed out and a star drawn onto their head. The shadows of passing clouds tiptoe through the window and drape across their sad empty faces and he remembers why they were chosen. His victims aren't random. Every one of them handpicked, chosen because of how special they've become to him. An agenda born of vengeance but doused in love.

He's waited long enough for this moment, years

of planning finally coming to fruition. It's perfect because he does so little to reap so many rewards. His victims are rendered defenseless and disarmed within seconds. The world that once rained the harshest blow on him now wraps its loving arms round him, keeping him safe and delivering the final blow to his victims. Just so he doesn't need to.

He turns to the door, licking his lips, wary of the time. He has somewhere else to be. With purpose in his gait, determination in his fists, the killer pulls on a white t-shirt and reaches for his car keys.

It's time to visit upon victim number three.

7.

Orange light spilled out from beneath the arches of Glasgow University, an illuminated block of gothic bricks spired into the misty sky. As she gripped the ice-cold bannister, Kate climbed up the stairs with the unyielding sense that she was being watched. Why hadn't she just gone home? Phil had also offered to pick her up, but she was keen to finish this meeting with her tutor and get home sharp. The thought of waiting around Alan Groundwater for longer than she had to was not an inspiring one.

Kate had never liked Groundwater. He was certainly more dynamic than some of the lecturers who had taught her, but his duality rather annoyed her. He spun between comedic figure in a handlebar moustache and a condescending patriarch too comfortable in his skin to be real. Kate was neither interested in his droll humour nor his overly confident delivery of the subject matter. Yet, here she needed his assistance.

Her heels clattered along the empty corridor, the echo grating as it filled the arched extension. The architecture was grand enough to have hosted true scholars but possibly too grand for today's rough and ready barrage of wannabe-minds. Kate didn't want to be a deep thinker, nor a great mind, rather settling for a career that would give her a decent income and a comfortable life.

Finally reaching Groundwater's office, Kate found the door slightly ajar. Knocking lightly, she waited for his invite to enter because, despite his inviting demeanour she sensed he still wanted his students to adhere to the commonality of good etiquette.

The rain suddenly began to fall hard, and she heard it on the window behind her. Kate turned to face the outside world, still waiting for a response from inside the room and felt a chill walk across her back skin. Little patterns formed on the window, partially shrouding the vision of a city fallen into darkness and hounded to silence by the impending arrival of Storm Maggie.

Something moved then; a shadow, the creaking of the door behind her and a figure leaned into her reflection. Kate spun, her ankle twisting and the cloth bag containing the rough draft of her essay rolled off her shoulder and landed on the ground.

'You are a nervous little tick, aren't you?'

Kate let out a slight scream. 'Oh my god, I am.' She let go of a nervous laugh, felt her face flush with embarrassment and grabbed the bag from the floor. 'Sorry, I don't know who I was expecting to find.'

He ushered her into the study, a room darkened by endless oak shelves full of dusty old books.

Kate had never been in here before and, despite herself she felt quite impressed. 'It's lovely in here. Is this where you work when you're not in class?'

Groundwater chewed on the end of an unlit cigar, moved behind a large Mazarin desk and perched himself on the edge. 'It's a risky night to be driving.'

'That's okay,' she replied. 'I'm a bus body. I haven't learned to drive yet.' She shifted awkwardly at the end of a brown leather sofa and adjusted her sleeves.

'Oh, you'll not get a bus tonight. The last one was at eight p.m. since the government issued the latest weather warning. Do you mean to tell me that you came here by public transport and that nobody told you there was no way of getting home?'

Panic rose in her. She certainly had no intention of bedding down in the university for the night. The place was eerier than an old graveyard when the bustle of people died. 'I'll need to call my fiancé. Do you mind?'

He shook his head. 'Though, I'm happy to give you a lift if you're not too far. Don't pull your partner out on a night like this if it's not necessary.'

Kate suddenly wished she had paid more attention to the news or listened in more to other people's conversations. She had taken the underground here and walked the short distance from Kelvinhall, never considering that there might not be a way out of the city. 'Honestly, he's probably still at work himself. I'll find out how far he is.'

'I insist,' interrupted Alan. 'You've nothing to be nervous of here, Kate. I won't bite,' he said with a wink.

Kate suddenly felt unnerved. She decided that a change of subject was necessary as she didn't want to focus on how uncomfortable she felt, or how much she detested the idea of being in a locked car with him. He had never said or done anything that should make her feel this way. Yet, being alone with him now only highlighted how intimidated she felt by him.

'So, was there something particular you wanted to ask me about?'

Her jaw lowered, her mouth agape and she ran her hands nervously across her trousers. 'Something particular?'

'The essay,' he laughed.

She suddenly felt stupid. That's why she was here, to get his help on the essay. He didn't offer his help often or freely and she'd been taken quite aback when he'd singled her out for this special tuition. Now she wished she hadn't felt so important. Still, here she was. Whatever was to come would come. Besides, she felt her nerves were possibly overtaking her. She let her shoulders slide and took a deep breath. 'I wanted to ask you about Infantile Psychosis as it's something that the latest essay instruction is asking about and I haven't ever heard you cover it in lectures.'

He ran the cigar under his nose and threw open the window behind him. A gust of wind battered against him. 'I find it rather tedious; truth be known. Less scholarly types want to box everything in, give it a title and be had with it.' He flicked a silver lighter and set flame to the end of the cigar, his cheeks sucking in as he inhaled.

'You teach psychology though. How can you not believe what you're teaching?'

'I didn't say I didn't believe it,' he asserted. 'I said I find it tedious. Do I believe in it? Yes, most certainly though I find it as interesting as dissecting a frog.'

She shuffled through her notes.

'Why are you asking about this? The final essay touches on the subject but its minimal comparative to the other subjects that you'll be theorising.'

'You know I started my placement today?'

'Yes,' he replied, and blew smoke through the open window. 'Did it go well?'

She nodded.

'But?'

Kate felt irritated that she was so easy to read. 'But I met a woman there who has a child who I think might be suffering from childhood psychosis. I've seen a traumatised child before but never anything like this.'

He stubbed the cigar out, moved round his desk and joined her on the sofa. 'You'll meet lots of children who are probably traumatised. Particularly in a refuge for abused women and children. Not all behaviours will manifest themselves in the same way.'

'There were lots of children there but none as bad as this boy. It was like he was having a seizure and then suddenly he just sat up and went back to playing with the toys. He also claimed there was someone outside watching him. When we looked there was nobody there.'

'So hallucinatory behaviour. That can be an indication of childhood psychosis, but it can also be the imagination of any six or seven-year-old child. Who didn't have a monster under their bed?'

'Mine didn't live under the bed. She slept in the next room.' Kate caught herself unaware because she hadn't meant to be so candid.

'Your mother?'

Kate flinched, gave a slight nod but realised it was a subject she didn't want to air in his company.

As if reading her mind, he returned to the subject she did want to discuss. 'So, you think this little boy has psychosis? Do you feel qualified to diagnose him?'

'I'm not sure,' she said, dipping her head in slight embarrassment.

'I'm not challenging you, Kate. I genuinely want to know how you reached your summation.'

'He just seemed,' she paused. '-muddled, confused, convinced he was in danger from this person he could see outside. The change though, it was sudden and-,' she paused, searching for her words. 'I don't know how to describe it, but I have read some materials on this subject and it just makes sense.'

'Perhaps what is happening to that little boy is that he's reliving some of what he has already endured. You've also got to remember that no two people will react the same way. Maybe one child is stronger than another. Maybe one mother is more protective than another. It's odds and sods.'

She laughed at the expression because it was so at odds with the rest of his vocabulary.

'Are you laughing at me? Or with me?'

'Both,' she said, feeling as if he had lifted the slight mist from within her.

'Try not to worry about it,' he ordered, casually. 'Your real concern should be with this essay. Have you done much work on it?'

She pushed the pile of paper across the table and for the next forty minutes they perused her every word, scoring through what he didn't like and scribbling in a frenzy what he felt should be added.

When they were done, Alan went back and closed the window. 'It's getting tough out there. Did you message your partner to collect you? That lift is still an option.'

'I didn't message him,' she replied, feeling quite apprehensive. She still didn't feel comfortable climbing into a car with him. Particularly when she thought of Phil's current investigation and how unsettled she had felt arriving here. She chastised herself for feeling so mistrusting because not every man was a predator and not every woman was a victim. Should she find herself in a situation that she wasn't comfortable with, wouldn't she be able to say no? Kate suddenly felt more vulnerable than she had in three years. In an hour's time she would realise just how silly she had been for being so paranoid. For now, her guard was up, and she was slipping her hand into her bag in search of something to defend herself should the need arise.

8.

The mist had devoured the entire sky. Only an army of orange streetlights could be seen for as far as the distance went. Such an ominous vision might have frightened some people. Not Charlie, because she had already endured the worst thing that could happen to her. Someone had already invaded her world without invite and she hadn't been able to fight back. The next bastard to try wouldn't be so lucky.

Charlie glimpsed at the road ahead, the fog draping just above ground level and drifting towards her. She was only thankful that much of the sleet had been washed away by an earlier downpour. It would make her walk to the subway station less perilous.

She reached into her pocket to ensure her pocketknife was still there. She ran her finger along the lightly serrated edge and felt a gust of relief for its company. That blade really was her best friend. Even though she'd never needed to use it, she never wanted to know the feeling of needing it but finding it gone.

She followed a set of dim lights in the nearby traffic, guiding herself along the edge of the pavement. She'd made this journey every night for the past two years. Routine was as key to her survival as anything else. For every terrifying scenario she could imagine, Charlie had also imagined an outcome; a jab to the chest that winded him long enough for her to attack, a knife to his back that would leave him to bleed out in the gutter. Just where he belonged. She had rehearsed every scenario if he ever found her, physically training herself to attack, or run because when the moment came, if it came, she might just lose her nerve.

Once she arrived at the subway station, Charlie

leaned against the rubber belt on the accelerator. *Don't ever feel safe*, she reminded herself. The lights were bright, the hustle a jolly. It would be remiss of her to assume nothing could happen to her in this throng. Some of the faces were familiar but not pleasingly so. She eyed a woman who always smiled but had never worked up the nerve to speak. Then a man who always seemed to be rummaging awkwardly in his brown satchel. Finally, before stepping onto the arriving train, she shrugged her shoulders nervously at an elderly gentleman who tipped his newspaper to his forehead.

Still never letting her guard down, but keen to avoid more eye contact or pleasantries, Charlie plugged her headphones into the jack of her mobile phone and hit the play button. She had deliberately snapped one of the wires so that the sound only came in her left ear. That way nobody would disturb her, but she still had one ear switched on to the world. She avoided eye contact from then on.

Charlie arrived home just after six p.m. Just like everything else, she had a process for her arrival. She unlocked the door and threw it open, trapping the pocketknife in the grip of her hand. She watched as the cardboard strip fell from the top ledge of the door confirming that the door hadn't been disturbed since she'd left this morning. Then she eyed the two aligned light switches at the bathroom door and threw them up. Her eyes tightened as the hall became illuminated and she was able to see that all the internal doors were exactly as she'd left them. She closed the front door, so it was only slightly ajar. She'd worked over this scenario too many times to lock herself in right away. There always had to be an escape.

Pulling the knife from her pocket she saw it glint against a silver mirror frame. Charlie then wrapped her other hand round a spray that she normally kept in her bag. She eyed the dark circles round her eyes, the trail of sleepless nights forever draped across her cheekbones. Her nightmares would forever be clotted by that terrifying night where her life had changed forever. He might have fought his way into her subconscious. It was the most he'd get from her now.

Charlie spun round holding the spray ahead of the knife. She kicked open her bedroom door and sprung the light. Nothing had been moved in there either. She repeated the process in every other room in the house until it was evident that nothing had been disturbed. Fear no longer paralysed her, but the twenty-minute cycle of preparation for every homecoming had long since frustrated her. Angry her life had come to this; Charlie kicked the front door shut and dropped a steel bolt.

Finally convinced she was as alone as every other time, Charlie let out a sigh and threw her bag and coat onto a black reclining chair. She then fell onto the sofa and ran her fingers across the scars on her chest. Once upon a time she would sleep there night after night, dreaming of revenge. She no longer plotted revenge or willed him out of prison. She hoped he died in there. Still, should the occasion arise Charlie was only too willing to rain down the same violence he had delivered on her. The only difference being she was intent on finishing the job.

9.

The scent of chilli wafted through the air as Phil rubbed his hands on the plastic apron. He made a mean chilli, even if he did say so himself. He was modest in most ways. Not about that. The radio played a cheery song that he always heard in the car and he found himself singing along even though he was sure Harry could write something more insightful and mature.

'When's mum getting home?'

'Soon,' replied Phil, adding a little more tomato to the pot. 'I think she'll be happy if your homework is done and we've got you bathed and ready for bed. What do you think, fella?'

Harry looked as if he were about to protest but must have thought better of it when he read Phil's stern expression.

When the boy disappeared, Phil lowered the heat on his latest concoction and opened two case files on the dining table. He kept his mobile phone within vision so that he was able to have it quickly to hand.

The files didn't have anything new. The pictures of the dead women were among the most graphic he'd seen in a long time. They weren't the most violent deaths he'd encountered but there was something cruelly sadistic about them, turned by the hand of someone with an evil calculating mind.

He went through the statements of those last to see both Michelle and Beth. There was nothing that stood out as particularly noteworthy. Yet, those people were the last to pass time with two women who would be snatched later that day and left to die.

Twenty minutes passed and Phil realised he hadn't heard from Kate since she'd left the refuge. It hadn't occurred to him until now but on the screen, he could see the newscaster delivering more on the current status of Storm Maggie. He grabbed for the remote control, adjusted the volume and listened as the woman jovially delivered a report on most of Scotland coming to a standstill. It was the section on commuting that caught his attention.

Harry wandered back into the lounge, now in his pyjamas and thrusting a workbook under Phil's face. 'Can you sign this for me?'

Phil pushed it aside. 'Give me a second, buddy.' He reached for his mobile phone, casually scrolling until he got to Kate's number.

'I need it signed for tomorrow. My teacher will give me into trouble,' whined Harry, seemingly unaware that the colour had suddenly drained from Phil's face.

Kate's mobile jumped to voicemail. Why hadn't she contacted him to ask him to collect her?

'Harry, I need you to go and change back into your outside clothes.'

The little boy looked at him with narrowing eyes. 'Why?'

'Now's not a good time to ask questions,' he said, patiently. 'If you just go and get your clothes back on, we're going on a little adventure.' Phil was aware he didn't want to panic Harry, but he also didn't want to feel panic himself. He dialled her phone number once more, hoping that she'd answer, and he could call off the mini-search party.

No answer.

He turned off the heat on the chilli, folded close his case files and rushed to the bedroom in search of his wax parker. He knew there was no reason to worry yet because bad weather didn't automatically mean that someone had fallen into danger. He reassured himself that Kate must have gone to her appointment with her lecturer and was probably keen not to have him and Harry go out in this weather. Would a night at the university really be so uncomfortable? Why wasn't she answering her phone?

He and Harry headed for the front door, both zipped up like mountain hikers in a snowstorm and ready to face the perilous winds. He was pulling the door open when a figure suddenly emerged from the stairs.

'Kate?'

Her hair was dripping wet, her clothes sodden from her short dash into the building. 'Oh my god, it's like Armageddon out there!' She was clutching her chest, breathing heavily and rushing towards him. 'Where do you guys think you're going?'

Phil felt all the relief he could muster, threw his arms round her shoulder and escorted her into the house. 'We were coming to get you, of course. Weren't we, Harry?'

Harry, unfazed by the entire encounter, simply nodded and shrugged. 'Mum, will you sign my homework? Phil was too busy to do it.'

'Why, you little clype.' Phil looked at Kate in mock disgust. 'I was phoning to make sure your mum hadn't gone on a shopping trip with all our money.'

She moved to the lounge, threw off her wet coat and slumped into the chair. 'Dinner smells so good. I could get used to this.'

'When have I got time to cook like this? If not for old Maggie showing her teeth, I'd probably still be out trying to solve what happened to Beth and Michelle.'

Kate's face changed.

'What?'

'Nothing,' she replied.

'No, what is it?'

'I got a lift home from Alan Groundwater, my lecturer. He really gives me the creeps. I don't know what it is, but there's just something off about him.'

'It's not like you to be like that about someone. Has he said something specific?' Phil's face formed a smile. 'Do I need to have a chat with him?'

'No. You know I'm usually quite approachable but there's something about him that gets right up my nose. That's not really what was on my mind though.'

'Then what?'

She sighed, grabbed a towel and shook it through her hair. 'For the first time since all that happened to me a few years ago, I felt unsafe. I just had this sense that I was being watched or followed. I didn't see anyone or hear anyone. It was just a feeling. Like an instinct.'

'Kate, you know you can phone me to collect you. You don't have to accept lifts from creepy strangers. I'd have driven over and picked you up. If you need to go somewhere from now on, just ask.'

She tusked. 'And be a prisoner again? I don't think so.'

He felt frustrated by her need for independence. Soon she would be his wife. He wanted her to be safe. He wanted to protect her. Did he really have the right to demand that she allow him to do that? He ignited the gas beneath the pot of chilli, gave it a quick stir and hoped that Kate's defiance would not be something that led her into danger.

10.

The killer slams the car door, walks through an iron gate and eyes a crypt far in the distance. Within moments of exiting the vehicle, his shoes begin to fill with rainwater, his lashes batting off salty rain. He doesn't notice such trivialities as the weather, other than to celebrate the opportunity storm Maggie has given him.

He holds the wooden bar in his hand, the sound of water hitting against the metal end and marches towards his destination.

Rising stones and damp bud-less floral arrangements spread across his view and he remembers the nights he would sleep here of his own volition. He's used to the outside because he has endured the worst of it. He survived because he had the tenacity and the will to live. He knew there was no-one to save him. His chosen four aren't so aware.

The moon arrives, shades of white and grey illuminating the dark passages whilst the wind carries branches that claw like a pride of lions.

The killer, undeterred by the lengthy drips of water down his arching back climbs a set of stone steps, past the spire atop a sleeping crypt and finally arrives where he wants to be. He brings round the wooden object in his hand, gripping it tightly so its end cracks the soggy ground. He looks at his watch, 9.05p.m. The perfect time to be here, long after visiting time, long before the witching hour.

Dirt splashes up his trousers, clutching at the threads like the fires of hell are rising to take him down. He barely notices, instead forcing another crack at the ground. He thinks of victim number three, firmly within his grasp now. He hopes she'll pose more of a challenge than the first two. In fact, he's counting on her. She'll put up the most fight but his number four, the final girl will be his most rewarding.

He widens the space beneath him, the muscles in his arms beginning to ache and he wonders just how far there is to go. A glance at a star, blazing but lonely and he knows that she is watching, smiling with approval. It's what spurs him on. Knowing that he's making this sacrifice so everyone will know her name. Being caught is not frightening to him. What frightens him most is that it would all be for nothing and that nobody would ever know what happened to her.

He looks down again and finally unearths what he came here for.

11.

Charlie lay awake and remembered when she used to patrol her house. Long before she'd found the resolve to fight, her only real ally was her eyes. Everything else had been defeated when *he* first entered her life and violated her. The one thing he couldn't violate was her ability to see things clearly.

Of course, her subconscious had also been her enemy once upon a time. Charlie had woken to the sound of her own screams on many occasions, the nightmares so vivid she could often remember them hours after they'd ended. The dreams were like an alternative reality, her same life with a different outcome. On one occasion, she had been standing in a courtroom, enveloped in silence and every set of eyes stuck on her as if they'd been glued into place. One had stood and delivered the verdict, a not guilty that had sent her spiralling into a frenzy. A would-be killer about to get his life back, laughing and winking at her as he walked to freedom. In the moments after she would wake, Charlie would have to re-adjust herself to the memory that he was languishing in jail where he belonged.

There wasn't a night that went by when she didn't think of him. She knew she was giving him more power than he deserved, a man who had penetrated her life without warning. He had taken the most valuable thing she had. It sickened her to think of it. Despite her determination to live this new unscathed life, she had wrapped her inner self in steel, her trust of every other person in the world now broken. Her body succumbing to a new fleet of rage, Charlie accepted there would be no sleep tonight. She got up and headed towards the kitchen.

The kettle whooshed until it grew to a bubbling boil. Her mother's motto had always been that tea fixed everything. Until they faced a problem that was too big to be fixed by tea alone. Still, as she warded off the scare of the battering wind, a cuppa would serve its purpose for now.

With a steaming mug in her hand, Charlie walked to the kitchen window. No matter how many times she reminded herself he was safely locked away, she still expected to find his rancid leering face glowering through the window at her. Finding he wasn't there was never a relief. He could be anywhere. *He's still locked up*, she reminded herself.

The only illumination inside the room was from a small triangle light underneath her crockery cabinet. She could see that the mist from earlier had lifted, the moonlight flowing freely across the clouds. How she longed for a time where she could wake in the night and only feel excitement for what the following day would bring. Now she waited for the first trickle of sunlight, so she could feel moderately safe again.

Her thoughts were interrupted by a tiny click. She moved her head slowly, cocking her ear towards the hallway. More noise, louder now, this time metal touching metal. Someone was at her front door. Her heart began to pound so hard she could hear it funnelling into her ear. She spun round, staring past the frame of the kitchen door, waiting for the main entrance of her house to burst open.

Had the time finally come for her to put her money where her mouth was? Had he finally found her? All that internal chatter about her right to defend herself when she crushed his skull in didn't deter her nerves. Suddenly, she wanted to run. Or check the barricade on the door. Had she remembered to put it on, she found herself wondering? A hundred different notions rushed through her head, none of them making any sense and only making the panic in her heart grow.

The door handle was creaking now. The lock was turning.

Charlie tried to remember feeling this frightened before. She hadn't had the chance when her assailant had broken in and violated her because she hadn't known he was there until he was on top of her. She placed her hand on her chest, concealing the scars as if she were protecting a new-born baby. Then she held her breath.

Finally, Charlie found her legs. There was a bat in the corner at the end of the hall, exactly where she'd put it. She fled towards it, ready to bring it down on the head of anyone who stepped into her safety zone. Her hands were shaking.

Suddenly there was silence.

Charlie dared not move more than an inch at a time because she could feel the terror escape every crack in her skin. Finally, she pushed forward just enough that she could eye through the tiny peephole. She squinted, adjusting her eyes to the darkness. The tiny tunnel was filled with light so she knew whoever had been there must have moved away from the door. It didn't calm her any. She lifted the steel bolt, listened to the dry rust as she turned the key and pulled the door slowly open. Her breath stopped. Just long enough for her to be afraid it might not come back. Sweat washed the nape of her neck, snaking down the arch in her slender back. One more glance and she stepped out into the landing. A look in both directions revealed there was no-one there.

As she hovered by the stairwell, clutching the

edge of her door frame, Charlie suddenly saw something move out front. A shadow passed so quickly that it could have been the reflection of a passing cloud. She moved, barely an inch but enough that she was departing from her door. Then she heard the back-door creak. Her face twisted in horror as she lifted the bat above her head. She was quivering, her breath shuddering inside her mouth. She didn't have time to look at his face. He was battling down on her.

As she heard her name being called, Charlie felt her sanctuary destroyed once more. She caught a glimpse of the hooded man, tried to bring the bat round on his broad shoulders but found herself screaming instead. He was at least six inches taller than her, a brute who could probably lift her and snap her spine with very little effort. Charlie had no more time to waste. She lifted the bat quickly and prepared to bring it down on his head.

12.

Standing on the steps of the church, cradled by darkness, the killer has been watching her house for the past half hour. He massages his aching arms and waits with inhuman patience. He has mastered the art of stillness a long time ago and it has become a servant to him. He watches, painfully watching as every light in the building is eventually snuffed out. Most intriguing to him is the one on the ground floor. The lowered blind only partially marks the silhouette of the young woman, the one he has saved for second-to-last.

One step forward and he's on his way. It's then he feels the adrenalin pump through him. It no longer feels like the first time. When he took the first victim, he wasn't a killer. In fact, there were moments where he didn't even know if he could go through with it. It wasn't fear, nor any sense of empathy with his victim. He had known that once the line was crossed, he would never be able to come back. A permanency he hadn't been sure he was ready for. Yet, once it was done, he discovered elation. A high like no other. Like the one he's feeling now.

Another step forward, ignoring the drone of a car engine in the distance. It isn't coming this way so no need to be concerned. There's a dim light that makes it a little easier for him to see her. He's close enough that he can see the steam from her drink. She takes a swig, pouring back her head like she hasn't a care in the world. He knows differently. He moves slowly, hoping for complete darkness because she won't be as akin to it as he is. He doesn't just like it, he adores it. The church behind him is a place for the godly to serve their master. The shadows are his master. He passes the pronged iron gates, his hand creeping into his pocket where the acid solution lives. A step off the pavement, the road barren of traffic or pedestrians, and he's approaching her building. He feels inside his pocket, feeling for the spray, a syringe and a set of cold metal car keys. As he looks up again, his breath catches, and he realises she's standing close to the entrance of the building. She must have seen him. He shifts out of the light, staring from beneath his hood, watching in anger as someone else comes through the back entrance. His breath quickens. Anger surges. Someone has beaten him to it. A moment later, as he rages silently about the man who is now reaching for her, he begins to feel fuzzy. He turns back to the green car still parked at the end of the street and begins to run. It should be his getaway car. Instead he's leaving empty handed. For the first time in months he feels his anger spiral out of control.

13.

At almost midnight, long after he'd sworn to Kate he was coming to bed soon, Phil ran his hands over the mountainous papers that were now gathered on the dining table. A stressful day had continued long into the evening, so he turned to the one thing that was ever faithful; *his work*.

Phil was running on empty. Whatever calories he'd devoured from his chilli were long gone, his stomach twitching in hunger. Rather than clattering round in the kitchen, he opted for a warm coffee and a chocolate digestive. Not exactly food for the soul, but enough fumes to carry him over the bones of a murdered girl's past existence.

The final days of Michelle's life were hazy. Beyond her work life, nobody seemed to have much of a clue where she went or what she did. Not even her own mother could enlighten them to the type of person Michelle was, only that she was kind and funny; attributes too often relegated to the dearly departed.

Another dart over the witness statements from those who had last seen Michelle, documenting that she had finished her shift at the bar she worked, necking a much-earned lemonade before departing into a grim cold night not unlike the one befalling now. It told him nothing. In fact, the only thing of interest in any of the statements was that of a friend who attested that Michelle had been seeing a man the year before. If only they had learned his identity.

'Who is your mystery man?' Phil stared into her eyes again, still moved by the emotion in her face, still mystified by the lost ghostly appearance of a girl who everyone had described as happy and fulfilled.

He moved to the crime scene pictures, clusters of little yellow numbers at various junctures. Not least disconcerting was the image of Michelle herself, her forever ashen face unable to move beyond the horrific branding and the melted look circling her eyes.

Phil rubbed his chin, stifling a yawn and convincing himself there was still something to find. Even though he knew his team had gone over everything with the tenacity of a Rottweiler he was sure they must have missed something. The second scene had been contaminated by Steve Carter's stupidity but there was nothing beneath his fingerprints that gave any insight into who the killer might be.

Another thought occurred to Phil then. No track marks from a car tyre had been found in the search, no footprints either. Somebody had to get Michelle Evans to her place of death and the weather had been so torrential for most of that week that Phil couldn't see how a person could avoid leaving some trace.

He leaned back and took a sip from his coffee. Then he dialled Donna's mobile number on his phone.

'Do you know what time it is?' She sounded too flat to be angry as her voice drifted back at him.

'Sorry, did I wake you?' Without waiting for an answer, he continued. 'How does a person trek through muck carrying another person without falling, or leaving a footprint?'

Donna sighed. 'I've wondered the same thing myself. I don't know is the answer. Maybe they floated.'

He snickered. 'Good one, Donna. Seriously though, it's like this person is a ghost. In those conditions, surely there'd be some evidence left behind.'

'You've got to remember that while they discarded her body in those conditions, we were also trying to work through the clues in similar conditions. Maybe we missed something. Or maybe there was enough time between them dumping her body and that caretaker finding her for the weather to wash away any evidence.'

'Forensics did identify the care takers footprints,' acknowledged Phil.

'Obviously he's not a suspect. He's seventy-three.'

'Yes,' agreed Phil. 'Old age is a very clever disguise.'

Donna cleared her throat. 'If I didn't know you better, I'd think you were serious.'

'I don't know if I'm serious or not. At this point, any lead is better than none.' He looked back at the reports on the table and shuffled them. There had to be something rational to explain the absence of evidence, something that didn't take them to the bank of the supernatural. They just hadn't looked deep enough.

'The one thing I'm sure of,' interjected Donna, '-is these girls aren't being murdered randomly. It's calculated. The killer knows who he's going after. Michelle Evans was virtually estranged from her family and had little by way of a social circle. It's very easy to make somebody disappear when nobody will miss them.'

Phil felt a shiver tingling at his spine. He had to agree that what Donna said made sense. 'Her limited contact with people makes it difficult for anyone to pinpoint who she was in a relationship with, if that was the case at all.'

'I also don't get the impression that it was done out of hatred either. There's nothing frenzied about it.'

'The killer has been very measured. That's why he's been able to cover his tracks so well.'

Donna went silent for a second, then her voice rose. 'Who took the picture?'

'What?'

'The picture from her birthday a few months ago. Her mother sent us it, but it couldn't have been taken by her because she said that they haven't seen each other in over a year.'

'It could have been anybody, Donna,' replied Phil, starting to wane from hunger and exhaustion. 'You know what it's like when you're in a bar and you ask somebody to take a picture of you.'

'Usually when you're in a crowd,' said Donna, matter-of-factly. 'People don't usually ask strangers to take pictures of them by themselves. That's why they've got a selfie function on most phones. Whoever she was out with probably took the picture.'

'How do we find them?' Phil knew he had a lot to learn about technology but even he suspected that finding the person behind the camera might be some other worldly task.

'I honestly don't know,' laughed Donna. 'To be honest, I don't want to think about it anymore tonight. I think you should get yourself off to bed as well. We're not going to get anywhere if we're shattered out of our heads.'

Phil ended the call, looked at the photo of Michelle when she was alive and took a sip from the cooling cup. Then he pushed it all away because he knew he was about to drive himself crazy. Whoever had taken that picture probably knew more than anyone else about Michelle's coming and goings. If only there was a way of finding out who they were.

14.

'Charlie?'

She was seconds away from bashing his head in when she heard his voice. She recognised it instantly and threw the bat to the floor. 'Garry? Is that you?'

He pulled down his hood and threw his arms up to ward off her next swing. 'Are you off your nut?'

Charlie moved round him and grabbed his shoulders. 'You nearly gave me a heart attack. What the hell are you doing sneaking into my house in the middle of the night?'

'I'm not sneaking in. You gave me a key last time I was here. Unfortunately, you've bolted the door shut so I was round the back trying to get your attention without waking the whole building up.' He looked at the steel contraption now abandoned on the hall floor. 'You're still bolting the place shut?' He followed her in and nodded towards the steel contraption now abandoned on the floor.

'Have you never heard of a phone?'

'I have, but evidently you haven't. Mum said she's been trying to phone you for days and you will not answer. Anyway, I thought you might be sleeping.'

'Not much sleeping goes on in this house. You should have told me you were coming. I'd have made up the spare bed for you.'

Since her attack, Charlie's fear never really evaporated. Still, this was the first time since back then that the fear was as crippling. She'd be happy to see him in a few minutes. She wasn't quite there yet.

'No need for that. The couch is good enough for me.' Garry's voice was hoarse, but he spoke in a gentle whisper as he slammed the door. He leaned in and threw his arm round her shoulder. 'You can put your big brother up for a few nights, can't you?'

Charlie smiled. It couldn't have come at a better time. She would never admit it to anyone, but she was feeling particularly vulnerable recently and her paranoia didn't seem to be levelling off. She hadn't wanted to bother her parents in Spain. She also hadn't had much patience for her mother's histrionics recently. 'Sure. I didn't know you were on leave. When do you go back?'

He led her into the living room, throwing up the light switch and planted himself on the edge of the sofa. 'End of the week. I've been staying with my buddy in Cumbernauld for a couple of weeks, but I think his wife was getting fed up with me. So, I thought who better to look up than my little sis. You really don't mind, do you?'

She didn't mind at all, though he had really given her a fright. She wondered if she should tell him how uneasy his arrival had made her. Perhaps the conversation was best left for the light of day. Right now, she was just happy to see him. 'I honestly don't. I'm happy you're here'

'Funny way to show how happy you are,' he said, rubbing the back of his neck. He grinned; a set of perfectly straight teeth encased in a mat of designer stubble.

Charlie laughed. 'Creeping into someone's house in the middle of the night isn't exactly going to get you a welcome home party.'

'No, I guess.' He threw his legs onto the sofa. 'So, are you going to get in touch with the folks?'

'If mum didn't threaten to fly home every time I don't tell her how great I am within five seconds of her phoning, I might speak to them more. Thankfully, she's not phoning as much now.' The truth was her mother phoned every other night, so much so that Charlie had bought a new all-singing telephone in order to screen the calls.

'Cut them a break. I know what happened to you was terrible but spare a thought for how they must feel. Mum is riddled with guilt and Dad is so damn angry all the time. I think if they didn't go to the villa, they might finally crack up.'

Charlie shuddered. She hated how her father looked at her in those first days after the attack. When she'd woken in hospital and saw how badly wounded her chest was, she'd had no concept of just how bad her attack had been. Seeing her parents and how distressed they were, it quickly came into focus for her. 'I know,' she finally said. 'It's not fair on them. They did nothing to deserve any of this.'

'You did nothing either,' he reminded her. 'There's no excuse for what that pervert did.'

'Anyway, let's change the subject. I get enough time with him in my head. Do you want something to eat?'

He shook his head. 'Can I smoke in here?'

Charlie grimaced. 'No. You can go outside. The place already smells bad enough with you here.'

He laughed. 'Charming. I'm off saving our country and you're telling me I stink.'

'You want tea at least? I just had one, so the kettle won't take long to boil.'

'Anything stronger?'

'Yes, but I'm working tomorrow. I'm not staying up drinking with you. Help yourself though.' She pointed at a cupboard in the corner. 'There's vodka, red wine or gin. I think there's lemonade in the fridge.'

‘Lemonade?’ He gritted his teeth. ‘I’m after the hard stuff, sis. You may as well just give me the bottle.’

‘Then you can get it yourself. I’m off to bed,’ she said.

Charlie didn’t know about him off saving the world, but she certainly felt safer knowing he was here. She would sleep easy with him in the next room. He was six years her senior, fiercely protective of her and had vowed he would rip apart anyone who ever hurt her again. She didn’t doubt it. With that in mind, she was able to relax and slip off into a real and long overdue sleep.

15.
22nd January, 2019

Storm Maggie hadn't reached its peak yet. Full of bluster and spreading in faster than a tornado, the media were reporting that it was only gaining momentum.

Phil stood in the centre of the abandoned crime scene, shining a small hand torch round the pit and searching for anything that may have been missed the first time. So far, so unsuccessful. Victim number two remained unidentified, her remains lying on a slab in the mortuary awaiting the moment where someone deemed her absent enough to be reported missing. It only re-enforced to him that the killer must have gone through a careful selection process, ensuring he chose someone who wouldn't be too sorely missed.

Whenever something like this happened, it almost made Phil ache to find a family for them. Whilst his own family hadn't been perfect, his relationship with his father sometimes volatile, Phil couldn't imagine how it felt to be so unmissed that he could just disappear and not have anyone worry about him. How lonely that must feel.

It was just after eight a.m. and Phil had dropped Kate off at the refuge for her second day. They'd both appeared less stressed this morning, Kate determined not to be intimidated by Natasha's big personality, Phil equally keen his body count should not rise to three.

'They should bring back the death sentence.' Donna had never made any secret of her belief that the justice system wasn't quite up to par but some of her views seemed positively archaic to him.

'Well nobody's getting humanely killed on my

watch. There's a system in place for a reason.' He didn't look for a reaction, hoping she knew him well enough not to pursue such a conversation. 'I'm still confused about the method though. He snatches them by disarming them, injects them with a substance designed to knock a person out and then leaves them to die at the hands of the weather. Why not just overdose them with the sedative?'

'That sounds almost too simple.'

'Then there's the brand to the face,' he continued, hanging his head over the iron grid.

'A star?' She looked up at the sky. 'An astrologist perhaps?'

'A maniac who reads the horoscopes?' He'd laugh if it wasn't so ridiculous sounding.

Donna sniffed and stepped into the path of the yellow torch light. She kneeled onto a large rock and ran her gloved fingers across the soggy undergrowth. 'It's not the most ridiculous thing we've ever heard.'

'What about leaving them here? It's unlikely that many people come to this part of the park. However, it's not out of the realms of possibility. Do you think he's giving them the opportunity to survive?'

'No,' she replied, through gritted teeth. 'He knows exactly what he's doing. He's chosen the coldest days of the year. Look at the skies. A roof was blown off a row of terraced houses in the East end last night. You're driving down the street, trying to avoid a flying trampoline. He's waited for this and I don't think it's over yet.'

Phil was about to suggest something else when his phone began to vibrate. 'Hello?'

'Phil, it's me.'

'Hi, Carrie. Tell me you've got a name for my second girl.'

'Absolutely. Do I ever let you down?'

Phil smirked. 'Not yet. Let's not make new bad habits.'

'You ready with your drum roll?'

He could tell her he wasn't in the mood for her dark humour today, but he had already bitten the face off Donna on the way over in the car. He could have justified it to himself because Donna was prattling on about Steve again. He could just imagine her rolling her eyes if she saw him give out to someone else today. 'Tell me.'

'Her name is Beth Phinn. She's twenty-eight years old. Likely dead within six hours, though it's difficult to specify for definite. There is certainly much less trauma to the body than there was with Michelle Evans.'

'What about the branding on her face?'

'Same again,' answered Carrie. 'Approximately three centimetres in diameter.'

Phil cupped his hand across his mouth and rubbed at his stubble. He then gave a wiggle of his jaw to try and inject some heat into his face. 'Any signs of a struggle, or any sexual contact?'

'There's been recent penetrative sex, nothing rough or any signs of forced entry. Oh, and the eyes have been attacked with the same solution as victim number one.'

Phil clenched his jaw at the thought of it, thanked Carrie and then ended the call. He eyed Donna as she moved back to join him on the North side of the manhole. 'Did you get all that?'

'The gist of it.'

He stepped beneath a nearby tree, eyeing the sombre sky and leaned against the bark. 'Look Donna, I'm sorry about earlier on. I shouldn't have snapped but you and Steve are really getting my goat up these past weeks.'

'Why do you care so much whether we get on or not?'

'I don't.' He didn't know why it bothered him so much, he just knew that each day had become more dreadful than the last. 'I feel caught in the middle. He's bending my ear about why you don't like him. You're bending my ear about why I do like him. It's exhausting. We've all got too much going on to get caught up in petty squabbles. I'm just asking that you give him a chance. Or at the very least, give me a break.'

Donna rested her hands behind her back and rocked her shoulders from side to side. Finally, she looked defeated. 'Fine, but I'm telling you I'm right about him. He's lazy, entitled and will end up getting either us, or himself into trouble. I still can't believe that crap he pulled here yesterday, and I can't believe that you didn't rip him to shreds.'

Phil rolled his eyes. 'It wasn't the time or place. If it happens again, not only will I rip him to shreds but I'll give you carte blanch to say I told you so as many times as you want.'

Donna smirked. 'I hope I never have to.'

16.

The killer has been walking the streets for the past two hours. He's stared into the face of a hundred anonymous women, varying ages, a variance of sizes. He could take any one of them, just whip out the spray and de-arm them within seconds and have them in his car. Would anyone notice? The crowds all walk with their heads down, peasants on their own thrones waiting for something to come along and colour their dull existence. Maybe he'd do it just for fun.

He stares at a young woman at an ATM, skirt too short for a night like this, make up caked on as if it's a second cloak. She may as well hand herself to him for all the attention she's paying to what's going on behind her. She slips her card into the machine and taps on the keys a few times until it shoots out a small pile of notes. On her way to a night out, he surmises. Or maybe not.

As she moves away from the machine, he remembers why he began this quest. If he closes his eyes long enough, he might see the face of a woman he has immortalised in his mind. With the memory comes the tears. He won't afford himself tears. So, he focuses on his quest, not for revenge but to honour someone who has been forgotten by everyone but him. He tells himself everyone will know her name.

He watches the young woman snatch her money and move away from the machine. She lifts a lit-up phone from her pocket and begins to walk. He could be frustrated by the lack of awareness for her surroundings but she's making it perfect for someone like him to come along and sweep her off her feet. Literally.

As he follows her, he remembers his real target

once again. He thought someone had beaten him to it, someone else with the same bullseye. Until he saw her today. He almost lost his breath with excitement when he saw her arrive at work. The stars are on his side again. He's chosen his four targets with precision. There's no deviation from that. He wants to tell the young woman to wrap up, it's cold out here. Maybe tell her to pay more attention to her surroundings, advise her she just had a lucky escape because her other fate might have been death at the bottom of an abandoned shaft. It's not time yet. In any case she's not the victim he chose. No substitutes. His sights are set firmly on Charlie Westmore and nothing is going to stand in his way.

17.
23rd January 2019

In his own setting, Alan Groundwater had seemed unremarkable. Now, towering over Natasha at the front door of Marina Cullen House, Kate could see exactly why he cut such an impressive figure.

He swept in, one hand balancing a box of donuts, the other cupping a 4 set of steaming hot coffees. 'I understand this is the way to your heart,' he boomed.

Natasha clasped her hands. 'We've not seen you round here for quite some time. Are you here to find out how your protégé is getting on?'

Kate fumed at the description. She had worked damn hard to get through this degree. She resented the implication that she was anybody's handy work.

'Not at all. I have absolute confidence that Kate is smashing it. I just thought I'd pop in. We've had a few of her students here and it seems rude that we're not more involved.'

Kate looked at the growing row of women and children now standing nervously along the side lines and realised how entirely inappropriate his presence was. She rushed to his side, snatched the donuts and ushered him away into the lounge. 'I don't know if you should just turn up like this. Some of these women can't even look at a man in the street without freaking out.'

'What? You think they'll feel threatened by me?' He was mocking her now, his handlebar moustache upturning at one side.

'You'll be amazed at what feels threatening to someone who has been kicked and punched for ten years by her loving husband. What do you want anyway? We don't have another session until next week.'

His smirk rose. 'You think I'm here to see you? That's sweet.'

'Well, aren't you?'

'Not entirely,' he teased. 'I am rather interested in your diagnosis of that little boy.'

'Really?' Natasha entered the room, arriving just in time to catch the turn in their conversation. 'And what exactly do you want to know, Alan?'

'Actually, I'd like to meet him. I've done a lot of research in the past about childhood psychosis. I even wrote a thesis on it once upon a time.'

Natasha turned to Kate and scowled. 'I don't think I emphasised strongly enough the importance of confidentiality.' She shifted so she was standing almost cheek to cheek with Alan. 'I assume you're asking about Danny Walton. Let me assure you there is nothing psychotic about his behaviour. Shame on you for trying to exploit a vulnerable child.'

'Exploit?' Though he looked outraged, it was evident that the expression was purely to mock her.

Natasha, quite bemused by both of them, snatched the collection of coffees from his hand. 'I'll take them, thank you. It's the least you can do for parading in here with no concern for the emotional wellbeing of that little boy, you pompous ass.'

Alan stuttered, his faux outrage turning to mortification. 'I mean, I meant no offence.'

Kate wanted to laugh. She swallowed the urge because she could see Natasha was still fuming.

'Go on, get out of here. Don't come without an appointment and bring better donuts the next time. They're as stale as that old jacket you're wearing.'

Alan stormed out, insulted enough that he looked fit to explode.

When he was gone and the sound of the door slammed at the end of the hallway, Kate waited to be shredded by Natasha. It hadn't occurred to her that she wouldn't have been allowed to discuss Danny with her lecturer. She was about to offer a feeble defence when Natasha burst in.

'The absolute cheek of him. Wading in here like he's not just a walking cock. And betraying your confidence for his own gain? You'd be well within your rights to report him.'

Kate felt herself taken aback. 'I thought you were going to tear a strip off me.' The raging red of her cheeks began to fade.

Natasha laughed. 'If he hadn't brought coffee I might have been tempted. Listen, I understand your curiosity, but I want you to remember you're only here for four weeks. I warn you only for your own good that you shouldn't get too involved or too attached. I've seen a lot of parents and children come and go here. I've even taken on a few of their problems myself. It never comes to any good.'

'You?'

'Yes,' she hissed. 'Only half my heart is made of stone. The other half beats just like yours. I've helped a few of these girls. Most of them have either ended up throwing it back in my face the minute I called them out on their bullshit, or they've ended up right back at square one.'

Kate felt deflated. She came here hoping to find somewhere that instilled hope, a new lease of life for those unable to find it out there in the big ugly world. Instead she was starting to wonder if it was just a desolate pass-through for those who didn't have the will to truly escape their past. It was a thought that would remain with her for the rest of the day.

18.

The last known sighting of Michelle Evans, before the discovery of her body was at the end of Calder Street. A neighbour confirmed what CCTV had already hinted at, that she had almost made it home. Except, nobody was able to confirm exactly what happened upon the moment of her disappearance.

'Why are you such a conundrum?' Phil leaned against the desk, wondering why she appeared to live the life of a ghost. As far as he could tell, Michelle had left Ireland a few short years before, rarely spoke to her family there and had very little by way of human relationships since. 'Are we any further forward with the photographer of this picture?'

Donna pulled her spectacles from her face. 'Nothing. I think we need someone who knows their way round a computer. Steve mentioned something about a mirror search. I switched off because the rest was a foreign language to me.'

'Steve knows how to search photographs online? Why didn't you say?'

'No, he doesn't. He said he heard someone talk about it once. He's about as clued up as us.'

'Can we ask someone in the IT department? Can I leave that with you?'

Donna nodded and wrote the instruction on her notepad.

'What about Beth Phinn?' Steve entered the room and leaned against the water machine in the far corner.

'That's what we need to find out,' said Phil, mildly irritated that Steve had interrupted his chain of thought. 'How are these two women connected? Did they know each other? Do they have an ex-boyfriend in common? How did they end up being killed so similarly yet in completely different parts of the city? There're a million questions, and almost no answers. That's what we need to focus on.'

'Any sign of sexual assault on Beth?'

Phil recalled the conversation he had with Carrie. It was one of the things he always dreaded when delivering the news to a bereaved family member. The only thing worse than telling them their loved one had been murdered was to tell them that they had been sexually assaulted. It always felt like piling an added layer of distress on to an already over peaking mountain of grief. 'I've still to get the final report but it doesn't appear to be the case. Michelle wasn't assaulted in that way so I'm doubtful the killer would have changed his MO.'

Steve moved to the battered old table in the centre of the new modern incident room and leaned across, so he was staring directly at the board. 'Do you want me on house-to-house again?'

Phil smiled. 'Yes. First thing tomorrow. I want you speaking to every neighbour in her street, everyone she worked with, any ex-boyfriends you can come up with. I want to know what Beth Phinn was doing the night she disappeared.'

Donna smiled as she rose from her seat. 'And me?'

'You're with me, obviously,' he retorted, dryly.

They were interrupted by Steve's phone jingling and he promptly left the room.

'Probably his hot date from last night,' said Phil, infusing a little humour into the otherwise frosty atmosphere.

Donna's gaze turned back to him. 'I'm saying nothing.'

‘That’ll be a first,’ he whispered, and smiled.

As they collected their belongings, the investigation room door swung back open. Steve pushed through, still cradling a silver mobile phone in his hand.

‘I’ve just had a phone call from Natasha at Marina Cullen House. She saw the photo we released of Beth Phinn.’

Phil’s ears perked up; his curiosity piqued enough for him to stop moving. ‘And?’

‘She knows her. Apparently, Beth was a volunteer at the refuge when Natasha started working there.’

Phil sighed. ‘Thank god. I was starting to think these girls didn’t exist before they were found dead. Let’s hope Natasha’s just the break we need.’

19.

From behind the haze, Charlie watched three silhouettes approach. It was much darker than she had anticipated outside, but she knew she had stayed too long. Why did she agree to meet up with Garry and his friend? All she wanted to do was disappear into the fog and slip home unnoticed. It was the downside to having her brother here, he would force her to socialise, despite her undying wish not to.

'Charlie?'

She grimaced as the figures stepped out of the shadows. 'Steve?'

'Hello, how are you?'

Charlie smiled, not sure whether to find the exchange awkward or be glad of a friendly face. It had been a while since she'd seen him. It was odd to see him with an entourage.

'This is Detective Phil Morris, and his partner Detective Donna Barclay. We're here on official business I'm afraid.'

'Oh, you're Kate's fiancé. Very nice to meet you. She will not stop yapping on about you.'

'It's not much better at this end,' muttered Donna, rubbing her cold hands together. 'Nice to meet you, Charlie.'

'You're here about poor Beth, aren't you?' Charlie hadn't really known Beth very well. She remembered that the girl had kept to herself, didn't say very much to her colleagues and didn't seem very comfortable with the residents of the refuge. 'I can't believe what's happened to her. Is there anywhere safe?' She felt a coldness spike through her, causing her to shudder and recall a memory that she wouldn't allow all the way to the surface.

'Did you have much to do with her when she worked here?' It was Phil who spoke now, seeming undisturbed by the growing gale around him.

'I really didn't. I only knew her to say hello to. She came and went without much fanfare. Nobody else seemed to know much about her and then when she was gone, nobody mentioned her again. I don't mind telling you it was quite a surprise to see her in the newspaper this morning.'

Phil leaned forward and handed her a card. 'I know you're probably keen to get home. That's my number if you can think of anything at all that might shed some light on Beth's comings and goings.'

'I will,' she offered. 'Unfortunately, I doubt I have anything to add. Obviously, if I do think of anything I'll be in touch.' Charlie smiled at Steve, the one man in Glasgow who had made her feel welcome when she'd first arrived. It was he who had given her the help she needed to start her new life. She'd probably never have gotten the job at the refuge if not for him. 'It's nice to see you, Steve. Hopefully you'll not be a stranger.'

'Me?' He winked. 'Never. It's just been a busy time. I'll catch you soon, sweetheart.'

As they disappeared into the building, Charlie felt the strain of her fragility once more. She really didn't want to go to a bar tonight. How could she cry off without having to listen to her brother's endless droning about how sad her life had become. She wasn't sad, she was prepared. If only he knew just what it had taken for her to get to this stage? She headed towards the street, clouds twisting frantically in the far horizon. It almost matched her mood.

With her mind made up that she would at least try to show face for her brother, Charlie pushed against the wind, unknowing that every step she took was being watched by a pair of malevolent glowering eyes.

20.

'Can you tell me what happened to her?' Natasha uncrossed her legs and reached for her coffee mug.

'How well did you know her?' Phil tapped his pen on the end of the chair, irritated because he knew that this should have been home time and that Kate would be waiting anxiously for him to drive her home.

'Not well. I took over the refuge a year ago from November past, she was only just finishing. She seemed very nice, a little quiet and kept a lot to herself. I got the impression her home life wasn't great.'

'What makes you say that?' It was Donna who spoke now.

'I heard her on the phone a few times. At first, I thought it was a controlling boyfriend. Eventually she told me it was her mum, always calling to see what time she'd be home, where she was going at night or who she was spending time with. Her mother was probably protective of her, but it did seem quite intense.'

Donna nodded. 'Obviously, you'll appreciate how devastating this has been for her mother.'

'That old adage that a parent should never bury their child. I can only imagine how terrible it must be for her. As I was saying, I'm not judging the woman. Perhaps she had her reasons for being overprotective. I can give you a list of a hundred reasons just from what I see coming through these doors.'

Phil rubbed his elbows along the arms of the chair. 'What about friends, or boyfriends?'

'As I explained, I didn't know her very well. She certainly never confided in me. I do know there was talk of a secret boyfriend. I only know that because I heard one of the other girl's teasing her. She got quite annoyed and it was the first time I'd really seen a reaction from her.'

Phil glanced at Donna, shaking his head. 'Was she angry?'

'Not angry, per se,' said Natasha, positioning herself against her chair as if she were settling back into her throne. 'She wasn't that type of girl. She was very mild mannered. So much so that I wondered what she was doing here? Albeit she described her mother as pushy, she seemed to come from a relatively calm background, and it made me question what it was that she was looking for here at the refuge.'

'How long did she work here after you took over?'

'Six weeks or so.'

'Why did she leave?'

'She didn't say. She just came in and thanked me for the opportunity she'd been given but said she wouldn't have time to volunteer anymore.'

'Did you get the impression there was more to it than that?'

'Honestly? No.' Natasha winced. 'I just thought we'd run our course for her. Maybe she'd found another cause. There was no bad feeling or awkwardness about it. These girls give up their time to volunteer here and many of them know they won't secure employment out of it. I'm grateful even if they only do one shift. Beth was here for a year before I started. I sent her on her way with a great big hug and the offer of a reference should it ever be required.'

'No disputes with any of the other staff?'

'Not at all. From what I can gather, they didn't

know her very well but liked her well enough.'

'That would fit in with what Charlie just told us,' interjected Donna.

'What about this girl?' Phil held up a picture of Michelle Evans. 'Did you ever meet her here?'

Natasha leaned forward and squinted at the birthday photo. 'Never seen her in my life. Is she the other victim?'

Phil raised his eyebrow. 'The first.'

'You need to catch this bastard,' said Natasha, anger lowering her voice to a whisper. 'We need to be able to walk the streets and know that we're not going to get bundled into a car and murdered.'

'I want to make it clear that we're not suggesting the refuge is in any way connected to the murders. It may just be coincidence that Beth used to work here. Without saying too much, there is nothing in the method of the killer that suggests it's a domestic issue. I would also ask that you keep what we've discussed to yourself for the moment.'

Natasha placed her mug on the table. 'Of course. Though, I must warn you that I won't have the safety of my residents put at risk. If we can't count on the police to keep us safe, we'll have to do it ourselves.'

Phil let out a slight groan. 'I can appreciate that is a concern. We've no evidence that the refuge is at risk. Our priority is public safety and I hope that you'll work with us rather than against us to maintain that.'

Her face softened, suitably convinced that they were all on the same page. 'Absolutely. Let me know if there's anything else you need from me.'

'Just keep an eye out for anyone hanging round that shouldn't be here,' instructed Phil. 'If there is a slim chance that Marina Cullen House is being targeted, I want to be one step ahead of this maniac.'

21.

The world was loaded with unknown dangers. That's the first thing Charlie had learned from her horrific experience. There was no corner bright enough, no lock solid enough and no knife sharp enough to make her feel completely safe. She had mentally prepared herself for the worst, but it never loosened the tight knot of dread that constantly accompanied her.

As she walked through the masses of students on Byers Road, she felt no safer than she would feel in a dark alley at three in the morning. Hidden behind affable smiles lay the potential for predatory intent. She would never allow herself to be the prey again. For a moment, she wondered if the many eyes that drifted past her might conceal a set of eyes with more than a passing interest. Feeling a shred of worry, she felt once again for the tiny sharp blade that had become her better half. The feeling that she was being followed hadn't left her since she'd left the refuge. If only she could shake it off.

Charlie entered the bar and sought out the cheerful holler of her brother. He was meeting a friend. He had all but begged Charlie to come along. What else would she be doing after a meagre slog at her airy-fairy job, he had joked? She'd only be sitting in the house jumping at shadows, watching the doorknob turn and terrifying herself to death. Why couldn't she put the past behind her, he had asked once again? She had wanted to scream in his face, wondering if he and her parents were programmed to continuously recite the same nonsense. Had he ever been violated? Had he ever known what it felt like to have someone not only take your body against your will, but also live inside your head without invitation?

Of course, he didn't.

'What can I get you?' Garry's friend, Tony rose from his seat and ushered her in.

Charlie squirmed. She hated to be touched. She also hated to show her weakness, so she smiled and slipped in beside her brother. 'Just a ginger beer if that's okay.'

'Light weight,' teased Garry.

'I'm working tomorrow,' she insisted, laughing awkwardly. 'Some of us don't get the luxury of six weeks off to nurse our hangovers.'

'Ouch,' he nudged her gently in the ribs. 'Anyway, I don't get hangovers.'

She smiled. 'Only because you're either hardened to it, or you don't stay sober long enough.'

They both laughed, the first genuine easing of her tension.

Charlie didn't want to mention that she was sure she had been followed here. She had been through all that before. Another awful thing that came with the aftermath of her ordeal was the constant reference to her paranoia. There was an expectation that she should tough it out, stop looking for problems and get on with her life. She hoped never to find herself in danger again, because she feared nobody would believe her. Every attack, mental or otherwise would now be attributed to her fear, the endless paranoia that someone was out there waiting to attack her. Even now, certain that someone had been staring at her when she left her home, she could not talk to anyone about it. Not even her own brother, who would rib her endlessly and imply that she just needed to get out more.

'You okay?' Garry broke into her thoughts. 'You seem pre-occupied.'

He'd noticed, she realised. Perhaps he wasn't so unperceptive after all. Maybe he did have some inclination to what she had endured. Could he see her pain? She was sure it was etched in every line on her face. 'Fine,' she finally lied. Then she jumped at the sound of the bar door slamming shut.

'It's just someone coming in,' said Garry, as Tony approached the table with three fresh drinks in his hand.

'Jack D for you, kind sir. Ginger beer for the lady. And a hard 'un for me,' boomed Tony, his pale face shadowed underneath the shine of his wild black curly hair. He threw back the whiskey chaser from his glass and then reached for the half-filled pint of lager he had previously been nursing.

Charlie sipped from the glass and allowed herself to fall into the background as Tony regaled them with stories from when they were both in the army together. Every moment felt like this night would never end as she wafted away the heat from a nearby radiator. Her eyes darted from a group of girls who laughed loudly at the bar to an animated couple who appeared to be entering that weightless territory of tipsy disagreement. There was also a plethora of single people dotted around the bar, each smiling away their troubles to an unsuspecting world or crying them into the bottom of their near-empty glasses. If not for drowning in her own anxiety, she might have found it in herself to feel sorry for some of the more pitiful figures hovering nearby. *Not tonight, Charlie.*

She so badly wanted her bed. Why, she often asked herself? Every night she climbed under the duvet, she was greeted by the monster under the bed or the demon in her head. There was no comfort there, no real genuine safety. She often likened the mattress to a net, hanging her precariously over all the things that ailed her and ready to snap under the heavy weight of her baggage. What then? What happened when she was plunged back into that nightmare?

A finger snapped against a thumb an inch from her face.

'Wake up, Alice. You're not in wonderland now.'

A snicker from the two men beside her.

Charlie turned. 'Sorry, I was just thinking.'

'Less of that,' joked Garry, casting a humorous eye at her.

She tried to bat away her irritation. 'Somebody's got to.'

He leaned towards her and gave her a wink. 'Don't take life so seriously. We're just out for a laugh. Are you sure you don't want a real drink?'

Charlie would love to down a bottle of wine. Or a bottle of gin. Or anything that would get her completely off her head. She could join in the laughter, forget everything that had ever happened to her and be the Charlie she barely remembered. For one night she'd be free of the life sentence she now served. Yet, she feared the one night she forgot herself would be the night he'd come for her. She wouldn't take that chance, so she kept her heckles up and stayed within the jail cell he had relegated her to. 'I'm fine,' she finally answered when it seemed like she'd debated the offer long enough.

'Killjoy,' said Tony, staggering out from behind the table with a hand rolled cigarette between his fingers. 'I'm off to get smelly. Are you coming?'

Garry gave a nod of the head. 'Give me a

minute.'

Charlie reached for her jacket. 'I'm absolutely fine, before you ask. I just want to get home. I've got a perfectly nice casserole in the slow cooker that's been calling my name.'

He lowered his head and smirked.

'What?'

His shoulders rose. 'Sorry, I thought you'd made that for me. Tony and I dove into it when he came to get me.'

'You had Tony at my place?'

Garry shrugged. 'Yeah, is that a problem?'

Charlie tucked her hair behind her left ear and leaned forward. 'Is it a problem? Yeah, it's a fucking problem.'

'Chas, turn the volume down. People are looking.'

Fury overtaking any sense of embarrassment, Charlie pointed at him. 'You're not staying at mum and dad's house. You're a guest. Remember that next time. You don't just invite people I don't know round to the house.' She could see his reddened face as he tried to keep the smile in place. She almost knew she was overreacting but the beat in her head just kept thumping.

'I'm sorry. I didn't think you'd mind.'

Her anger clamoured into the centre of her chest and she let out a great gasp as if releasing her demons upon him. 'Didn't think it mind? Not good enough. You've got no idea, have you?' A tear appeared on her cheek and she felt it tickle at her heated skin.

'Not this again, Chas.'

'Sorry if my trauma makes you uncomfortable,' she snapped. 'Just because you swoon in like the big hero doesn't mean the world's suddenly a safer place.

You don't get to disregard all the things I've done to keep myself safe. And you don't get to invite strangers into my house.' She grabbed her bag, now becoming aware that all eyes were on her.

Garry rose. 'Chas?'

She was fleeing the bar, realising the heat wasn't responsible for the spreading rash of red across her face.

'Chas?'

She wanted to turn back, to scold him once more or to apologise for her unjust anger. She knew it should be diverted elsewhere. Perhaps on to the man who had given her cause to unleash her temper on her own brother? Still, he should have been more sensitive. She pushed past Tony in a haste when he appeared in the doorway of the bar. Her tears were flowing now so she didn't feel she could stop and say her goodbyes. Instead, she ran the short distance to Hillhead underground and fled into the safety of its brightly lit platforms. How ridiculous she now felt.

In that moment, she remembered the face of her assailant. She wanted to spit at him, even lunge at him with her hands clawed into weapons that would rip his throat to shreds. He wasn't there. There was no fighting a memory. For once she wished she had drained the drink from her brother's glass. Once again, she considered that maybe getting off her head was the only way to escape her never-ending nightmare.

22.

Kate still felt bothered by their afternoon visitor as an Italian waiter escorted her into her seat. 'Sorry I'm late,' she said. 'Natasha can fairly keep you chatting.

'Hey, no apportioning blame here. You look beautiful.' Phil stood, gesturing her into the seat as the waiter stepped away.

'Are you joking? I've seen badgers that looked less wild.'

Outside the crowds were dwindling, finally taking heed of the current weatherman mantra that they should batten down the hatches and prepare for the crisis. Kate wasn't to be as easily deterred considering how many weeks it had taken to get a reservation at Olive's.

'I phoned ahead and ordered the lobster. I thought it would be nice to try something new and celebrate finally setting a date.'

Kate lifted her shoulders with excitement. 'Setting a date? I don't think I set a date the first time I got married. One minute I was pregnant, the next we were standing with two of his work mates rushing through some vows the celebrant had printed off the internet.'

Phil laughed. 'There's no way you're doing that this time. I've already started writing mine.'

'You've got to be kidding,' screeched Kate, throwing her hand to her mouth as she realised a couple nearby had turned to scowl.

'Kate, I could live another fifty years and not have enough time to tell you all the ways that I love you.'

She kept her hand to her mouth, gushed with emotion and shook away the feeling that this was all just a beautiful dream that might end any day now.

Minutes later a bottle of Chianti arrived at the table, then a Dorset blue lobster served on a bed of mixed leaves with Rosemary and orange.

Phil looked positively queasy, his eyes rolling back as the waiter laughed.

Kate whooshed. She had never had lobster either but could acquire a taste for anything. 'It looks amazing.'

Her husband-to-be didn't look so sure. He snatched up the glass of red, took a thick gulp and rolled his hand for the waiter to hurry the serving along.

As the merriment continued, neither Phil nor Kate were aware that they were being watched by someone across the road. A figure with deep menace in his eyes, his evil intent not held back by something as trivial as Scotland's worst storm in nearly five decades.

'I don't fancy the drive home tonight, do you?'

The wine had already gone to Kate's head and she found herself giggling at almost nothing. 'How much wine have you had?'

'A small glass,' he admitted. 'I'd say I'm probably just a tad over the limit.'

She smiled. 'I'm a lot over the limit but I wouldn't say no to a nice plush hotel.'

'I don't know about plush,' he smirked. 'I was thinking the Western Barn at the bottom of the road.'

'That'll do,' she said, her eye suddenly catching sight of someone she knew.

'What's wrong?'

'It's him,' she said, her eyes following the man out the front door of the restaurant.

'Who?'

She watched him wave down a black taxi, turn back just long enough to make eye contact and deliver a sly wink. 'Alan bloody Groundwater.'

Phil bent round in his chair, but the taxi was already pulling away from the kerb. 'Your lecturer?'

'The one and only. Do you know the smarmy bastard turned up at the refuge today, deciding that he's interested in childhood psychosis after all?'

'Must have been a slow day in the world of psychology. Why are you letting him get under your skin?'

'I don't know. He flirts endlessly with students, male and female, loves the sound of his own voice and then had the audacity to break my confidence today. They're only the reasons I can remember. Ask me again when I'm sober.' She felt angry yet didn't know why he was having such a passionate reaction to him.

'I think you should give next week's lesson a miss if he gets to you in this way. Why would you want the help of someone who you have such little respect for?'

Kate didn't know. All she did know was she wasn't swayed by his flirtations. She had considered that perhaps she was trying to deny an underlying liking for him. She knew now that not to be true because his behaviour disgusted her. It was completely inappropriate and an abuse of his position. The truth was she simply didn't trust him.

'Come on, you. Let's get you to the hotel so I can take completely advantage.' He handed the waiter two fifty-pound notes and rushed round to help Kate out of her seat.

She was still ranting quietly about the elusive Alan Groundwater, incredulous that he'd dared to come to the refuge. 'He could have really gotten me into trouble, you know?'

Phil nodded agreeably, keen to get through the falling torrents and dry off at the newly opened Western Barn. 'Okay, beautiful. Let's get you out of here.' He glanced at the waiter, urged him to keep the change and buttoned up his jacket.

They crossed the road, preparing to walk down the quieter side of the street, neither aware that a few minutes earlier they were being watched by a killer. Nor that he had now disappeared from that place of voyeurism into territory much more dangerous.

23.

Charlie's anger had subsided now. As the icy wind blew through her, chewing at her chin and cheeks, she could see her home in the distance. The tears had subsided, pity party for one now calling time. The urge to drink, which had appeared quite resolutely when she fled the bar had been buried away in the back chambers of her mind. She'd been there once; she wasn't going there again. The urge to scream was a different story. Give her an abandoned field under a black sky and she'd let rip. Sometimes being in the city was too restricting.

She thought of her brother, humiliated by her outburst and probably feeling he was no longer welcome at her house and she wanted to call him to make her apologies. He shouldn't have violated her safe space. Where else could she let down her guard? He should have known better. Anger simmered just below the surface, but she wouldn't allow it to fully boil.

As she ploughed forward, wanting to rail at the Gods for their little part in the destruction of her life she could see the kitchen light so vividly that it restored a little of her faith. She was almost home, out of the cold and out of the way of predatory eyes. Time to put her paranoia in the same place as her abandoned alcoholism.

A moment later, Charlie unlocked her front door and carefully did her usual checks. Light switches thrown, doors checked, curtains undisturbed, right hand cradling her pocketknife and left hand reaching in for her spray, she finally let down her guard. Nothing to see here. As expected, her brother had left the lounge looking like it had been turned upside down and tipped out. Charlie was in no mood to clean it tonight, so she snuffed out the light and headed for the en-suite bathroom.

The steam rose from the hot water instantly. Charlie placed the pocketknife on a glass shelf where it would remain dry, hung her towel over the top of the shower door and carried her mace spray into the shower with her. Nobody was coming for her, she reassured silently but she would never be unprepared again. She stepped into the small square cubicle and threw back her head. The water splashed on her face before stealing through her hair and flattening it to her scalp. She fished a bottle of shampoo from the collection of potions at her feet, squeezed it on to her hair and allowed the sting in her eyes to conjure the memory of her eight-year-old self. She would give anything to be back there again, the horrors of this world not yet tainting her.

A moment later, the scrubbing of her hair stopped as Charlie heard a loud clatter, steel hitting steel. She froze, praying her brother had followed her home after her hasty exit. She reached forward and pressed the off button on the shower. It took a moment for the water to stop swishing through. As silence fell upon her, Charlie felt as if her brain was beating against her skull. She turned to face the inside of the bathroom, waiting for the slightest movement of any silhouette. She felt stupid now. Why didn't she just bring the pocketknife in to the shower with her? She wiped the condensation from the door, eyes darting round the small square bathroom. Her heart thumped against her chest. She cursed herself then, because she must have forgotten to close the bathroom door. It lay half open which was fine, because she couldn't remember closing it or locking it.

Charlie slid the shower door just enough to grab her towel and squeeze through it. Her heart was still pounding, her nerves ticking like the sound of the old wall clock in her bedroom. She moved her head slightly so that the sink on her left would come into view. It only took a moment to notice that the pocketknife was no longer on the shelf. She threw her hand to her mouth. Somebody was in her house. They must have been in her bathroom. She could hear her breathing shallow. In all the days and nights she had spent preparing, Charlie hadn't allowed herself the luxury of real exploding fear. It wasn't asking her now; it was descending upon her without permission. She turned her head the other way and then peered towards the half-opened bathroom door. The scent of lavender drifted up from inside the toilet bowl. It was nowhere near strong enough to eradicate her terror.

However ready Charlie thought she would be for this moment; it was evident now that there was no getting ready. Her thoughts drifted to her assailant. Had he gotten parole? Escaped? How had he found her? She had done everything in her power to make sure he'd never find her. Yet, here she was, certain she had an intruder. It couldn't be her brother. He would know better than to come into her bathroom when she was showering, wouldn't he? She wanted to call out for him. She couldn't find her voice.

Charlie stepped forward and suddenly felt ridiculous. Inside the sink lay her pocketknife. It had fallen from the shelf because she'd obviously not placed it there properly. How stupid she had been. She placed her hand on the centre of her breasts and allowed her breathing to calm. Her heart rate began to steady, and her brain no longer felt like it was going to explode out of her head. She reached for the knife and placed it back on the shelf, this time ensuring she pushed it towards the wall.

Feeling confident that she was already feeling better, Charlie decided not to go back into the shower. She'd had enough excitement for one night. Something else had begun to bother her though as she ran her hand across the mirror was that her breathing still sounded heavy. Her chest had settled, but her breathing still sounded raspy and forced. She hadn't realised just how frightened she must have been. Deciding that holding her breath for a few seconds might help, she took a lungful of air and lifted her shoulders. It was then she suddenly felt her fear return. She was holding the air in, but she could still hear deep breaths from around her. Charlie didn't even have a chance to turn. Nor could she scream for help. She caught a glimpse of a single eye in a small clearing on the mirror as a hand wrapped itself round her mouth and a tiny bottle rose up to release a vapour across her upper face.

24.
24th January 2019

It was the fading roar of the old jalopy that brought Charlie back to life. As she crawled to her knees, her fingers sliding into the mud, she was instantly enveloped in the eeriness. The winds howled like screaming banshees, yet she may as well have been suffocated in silence. She could hear the whooshing and clanking of machinery in the near distance though wasn't sure exactly what it was.

The rain battered down, matting her hair to her skin and lashing at the curve of her back arch. The drops felt hot, like globes of fire falling on her aching body. Her eyes, she realised were also burning though the pain hadn't been quite as instant. Now almost completely alert, the agony round her eyes grew more intense by the second until the only thing she could do was scream in agony.

Charlie pushed to the edge and pressed her hands against soggy wood. She listened more intently now, realising the sound of the car was gone. If only she could see as clearly as she could hear, she might well find some way to safety. She rotated her feet in the murky puddle and leaned against one of the wooden beams, realising now that she was completely naked.

'Oh my god!' Her voice rose to a wail, her throat constricting against the sound of her lonely cry. *He'd done it again*, was the only thing that passed through her mind. She listened for the sound of his breathing, a sound that had never left her in the years since he'd raped her. Her mind looped round all the questions that she didn't have an answer to. When did he get out? How had he found her? The only people who knew where she was and that she went by her mother's maiden name was her own family. Who would have told him? Charlie wailed a little more because she had spent these past two years preparing herself and when he finally showed up, she barely whimpered.

Charlie spent the next two hours marauding her thoughts, counting endlessly to block out the pain but every movement felt like an assault on her body.

Finally, able to climb to her feet, she could hear the squelch of the sodden mud as her toes dug in. It was then the anger penetrated. Not at him, not yet, but at herself for allowing herself to fall prey to him again. The first time had been an accident, this time was stupidity. As she tried to think, put a plan into motion, all she could really feel was the rain continuing to batter her until she was sure she must be red raw.

How long had she been here anyway, Charlie found herself wondering? Long enough that she was starting to feel the pull in her chest from the dip in her temperature. Long enough her skin had been ravaged by the elements.

Daylight slipped through silver clouds. Though she couldn't open her eyes fully, one little slit had formed in one and she was able to see that it was no longer dark. It was also enough for her to do a quick scan of the giant drum she now found herself in. The realisation she was completely alone both terrified her and gave her hope in equal droves. What terrified her more though was that the top rim of her prison revealed just how far below ground she really was. No amount of mental or physical preparation would be enough to defy gravity. With that knowledge she pummelled the depths of her chest and drew breath. Then she screamed so violently she would sure her ears were exploding. For a moment everything else fell into silence, as if stopping to listen to her cries. As she fell into the mud, reaching for a soggy wooden panel at the side of the rotunda, she finally tasted the salty grains of defeat.

25.

Daylight has finally emerged, and he's driving through the back roads to East Kilbride. The sun, whilst not exactly vibrant is bright enough to create a glare on the old car's windscreen.

The sound of Deep Purple blares from the ancient cassette machine, probably the only tape that still works, carrying him to a time filled with so much hatred that it almost eclipses any love he might have once felt.

He drives through the nothingness; the rain still pelting and wonders why he doesn't feel elation. Only sadness, perhaps because he knows it's almost over, or really because he had expected more. She was to be his equal, the one that would put up the most savage fight. He expected more than a gasp before she descended into the unconscious. She'd barely managed to free herself from his grip before he injected the sedative into a vein in her neck.

He'd waited for hours, staring into that large oval space, waiting for her to stir. He so badly wanted to tell her everything. He wanted to pour the truth upon her, the powerful gust of enlightenment. She would know everything he had endured, all the things that had driven him to this.

He's not an evil man, he reminds himself. Just a vengeful one. Taking from someone else what was once taken from him.

As the next song begins, it takes him spinning back to another age, one he recalls all too vividly in his nightmares. The last star sparkles above him, his imprisonment defied by the serenity of the moment. He can hear the distant voice of an angel, singing to him, comforting him and giving him hope he'll one day be free.

That day can't be far now. As he leaves the broken tarmac of a long-forgotten road, slipping into the onslaught of traffic, the memory changes to something far more encapsulating. So breath-taking is the leer of his abuser that he is forced to pull his car over into the hard shoulder. In that moment, he's no longer a killer, but a boy who is just about to feel the wrath of a leather belt. Thirty-four times, one for every morsel of food he has stolen.

He leans forward, resting his head on the old battered wheel and it's only then he can feel the release of anxiety. Tears form, like little slithers of memory, each containing one more reason for him to be vengeful. He's not ready to let them go yet. One day, when he's truly free, those tears will be discarded like the songs of old forgotten time. Not now.

He turns the key and puts the car back into gear. A moment later, he's safely among the anonymity of a hundred commuters and stiffening at the enormity of what he has finally done.

26.

Phil met the black-eyed gaze of an army of stuffed toys as he entered the room. The walls were disorientating, a gallery of heavy rock bands marrying a bridal party of evil Disney Queens. The bed was a further contrast, a floral spread that remained ruffled and unmoved since the first time they'd visited.

'It looks like the bedroom of a teenager,' suggested Donna.

Phil took a deep breath and tried to fathom exactly what type of person really did live here. They hadn't really ventured into the bedroom the first time, offering to return later when Marilyn Phinn became too hysterical for them to continue. He turned and saw the woman skulking in the hallway.

Donna walked ahead, tucking her hands into a pair of latex gloves. 'It's as if someone zapped her out of this room ten years ago and it hasn't been touched since.'

Phil tried to blink away the dull ache at the centre of his head. 'Donna!' He nudged his head in the direction of the door, a silent warning shot that the mother of a dead girl was hovering in the background.

Donna turned to Marilyn and smiled gently. 'We'll try not to disturb anything.'

'It doesn't matter,' muttered the woman, her voice like the echo of a ghost. 'Whatever you do, my daughter will still be dead.'

Phil moved to the window which was positioned at the back of the maisonettes and could see into the heart of the city centre. This was the view that Beth Phinn saw every single morning of her life. He looked down and saw his car parked in the private parking area. 'Is this the only place cars are allowed? Or is there parking on the other side of the building?'

Marilyn placed her front toe across the line of the door, edging dangerously close to entering the bedroom. 'That's the only parking for the people who live here. Why?'

'Do you mind if I ask where your bedroom is?'

She frowned. 'Why?'

'Does the window look out into the same area?' As he turned away from the window, he caught sight of a wooden board full of photographs.

'Yes,' answered Marilyn.

'Did you ever see her being dropped off late at night by anyone?'

'I would see her getting out of her taxi sometimes. I didn't sleep very well most nights, particularly not until I knew she was home safe.'

'So, you would wait for her?' He continued to eye the montage of photographs, still conscious of how lonely she appeared. Where were the friends? The lovers? The other revellers who should have made up part of this girl's story. Instead, every picture was a selfie of an isolated girl documenting her own bare existence.

'Isn't that what you do for your children?'

Now when they're nearly thirty, he mused to himself. 'So, you would worry about her? Can I ask why?'

'Because that's what you do when you're a mother,' she emphasised, clearly re-iterating her previous sentiment.

'Absolutely,' said Donna, now firing her very own warning shot with a glower of the eyes.

Phil felt immediately apologetic. Had it seemed like an attack? He would certainly never attack the parent of a dead girl. He turned away from Beth because the images were starting to make him feel sluggish, like Beth was drawing the breath out of him. Why did this room seem so constricting?

'Marilyn, do you mind if I ask you how you knew it was a taxi dropping Beth off? We're on the seventh floor here. Your eyesight would have to be pretty good to see all the way down there.'

Marilyn finally moved to the room door, her pale blonde hair floating behind her, dark circles ageing her face from when they'd first met her days before. 'I don't. I trust,' she paused, clearing her throat, '-trusted my daughter. If she told me she'd taken a taxi home, what reason would I have to distrust her?'

'Kids can be secretive,' said Phil. 'Maybe she didn't want you to know if she was seeing someone? Maybe she didn't want you to worry?'

'Then she failed,' replied the women, fuming bitterly.

'Did she ever mention any male friends?'

Donna stepped forward. 'Or female?'

'What are you asking?' Marilyn wedged herself in the door frame, her face illuminated by the cold white light from behind. Her eyes blinked furiously.

Phil scratched at his forehead once more, his headache growing more painful by the minute. 'Are you aware of anyone your daughter might have been in a sexual relationship with?'

Marilyn, immediately defensive, seemed to jolt forward. Yet, she still didn't enter the room, as if some invisible force was keeping her on the other side of the door. 'Your colleague told me Beth wasn't sexually assaulted. Are you telling me something different?'

'Not at all,' said Phil, quickly. 'However, the manager of the refuge where Beth volunteered has brought to light some information that suggests Beth may have been in a relationship that she was being secretive about.'

Marilyn paled. 'I'm not aware that my daughter was seeing anyone. Don't assume that I'm not aware Beth may have had flaws. Or may have lied to me. I lied to my own parents more times than I can remember. I was six months pregnant with Beth before I told my father. So, if you're asking me if it's possible she was in a secret relationship with someone, I'm not going to say she wasn't. I cannot, for the life of me fathom why she would feel the need to be so secretive.'

Phil was now convinced that Beth had gotten involved with someone who may have been responsible for her death, someone who may have sought her out and groomed her. The thought sickened him as he took a glance at the photo gallery once more. 'Would you say you and Beth were close?'

'No,' answered Marilyn, clearly not in the mood for pretence.

Donna took her turn at the foot of the photographs, shaking her head at the tragic loss that lay before her.

Marilyn cleared her throat again, her voice softening. 'Not for the want of trying. I was besotted with her. As a child, she was an absolute dream. Pretty, well behaved, clever at school, just the perfect child. I never had sleepless nights over her until she was nearly twenty. We just seemed to drift apart.'

'Why do you think that is?'

'If I were to hazard a guess, I'd say I was too clingy. We're not quite *mommy-dearest*, but I think she found me possessive. I couldn't help myself. I was young when I brought her into the world. My parents were in their late thirties when they had me. I remember being embarrassed by how old they were, so I thought the smaller age gap between Beth and I would make us best friends. How wrong was I?'

Donna shifted to her side. 'You weren't wrong, Marilyn. I bet you and Beth would have been amazing friends. We're all like that when we're younger. I was forty before I stopped being mortified by my mum.'

Phil noticed a shift in Donna's expression, one that started out as sympathetic but changing to sadness as she continued.

'You don't have to make me feel better,' said Marilyn. 'I'm not blaming myself. I'm blaming the bastard who took my daughter away from me and robbed me of all the years I'll never have.'

'We'll get him,' promised Phil.

'Will you?' She snorted in disbelief, floating away from the bedroom door. 'Will you be much longer? I'd really like to be alone now.'

Phil felt his phone vibrate in his pocket.

'We'll be done in a couple of minutes. We just want to have a quick look round her bedroom. There might be something here that could help.' Donna turned back and headed for a small bedside cabinet. She moved closer to look at a collection of costume jewellery and a bottle of perfume but there was nothing else of interest in there.

Phil listened intently to the voice at the other end of the phone, holding his free ear to block out the growing thunderstorm. 'I understand,' he finally said, hanging up the phone.

'Who was that?'

He smiled. 'I think we've had a breakthrough. A

small one, but it's better than nothing.'

'Oh?'

'A hair,' he said, lowering his voice. 'They've found a single hair on Beth's head that doesn't belong to her. Obviously, they must run tests, but it might be just enough for us to get a positive ID before this psycho moves on to someone else.'

27.

Garry didn't remember how the fight had started. One minute he was in the bar drinking with Tony and Charlie, the next a bouncer was kicking seven shades of blood out of him. Tony, good old friend that he was, was long gone by the time the first punch flew.

'Charlie?' He pushed the door open and saw her bedroom door was open. She must have gone to work already. That was good, because he didn't think she would appreciate him rocking home past breakfast time with blood tripping from his purple eye. He called her name once more, just to be sure she wasn't skulking in the house and refusing to speak to him.

There hadn't been many things that made Garry feel real guilt. Not being there for Charlie when she had endured the worst attack of her life had probably been his biggest. He could still remember the moment his father had taken him into the kitchen and broke the news to him. He had replayed the word 'rape', over and over in his mind, hearing it echo amid perfectly ordinary sentences until his rage had ravaged him.

A peak in the mirror revealed exactly what Garry already knew. His face wasn't his own. The upper left of his forehead was so swollen he thought it might grow another pair of eyes. His right eyelid had closed so only a bloody slit remained in sight. He was barely able to see where his own skin colour ended, and the ferocious bruising began. 'Bloody fine mess,' he muttered and ran a face cloth under the freezing cold tap.

When Garry had wiped away the debris from his cuts, flushed what little of the running blood still existed and assumed the only breakages were a couple of his aching ribs, he hobbled to the sofa and grabbed for a ruffled tartan blanket. He would message Charlie and tell her what happened, so she didn't come home and die of fright. He also wanted to apologise for the insensitive way he had spoken to her. Garry had always assumed he felt as bad as Charlie did, now realising his male ego had led him to that summation. In fact, he now knew he couldn't possibly know what she must have endured. No wonder she was so damn angry. An apology was the least of what he owed her. He pulled the blanket to his chin, feeling like he might implode if he moved another muscle, and drifted into an uneasy drunken sleep.

28.

From what she could tell, her attacker hadn't laid a finger on her. Not in a sexual sense anyway. Charlie remembered all too well what it felt like to be violated in that way. There was nothing about this that seemed the same. Yet, she still felt dirty.

Charlie had spent the last hour cupping up filthy puddles of water and rinsing her eyes with them. She could feel bulbs of gravel against her cheeks, yet the puddles seemed to have eased the pain. She couldn't remember fighting back and had chastised herself many times for it but there was a sense that her eyes hadn't been attacked as fiercely as she might have expected. Perhaps he'd only meant to disarm her long enough to render her unconscious.

Now able to determine shadows, if not fully regaining her sight Charlie crept across the mud and grabbed onto a piece of thin broken wood. She could hear the whistle of the returning storm, the machinery that she'd heard earlier now silenced but that didn't concern her now. She was deep enough inside the rotunda that she doubted the winds would even find her. Right now, Charlie's focus was saving herself. If she hadn't defended herself in the way she'd promised, next time he wouldn't be so lucky.

Whenever Charlie felt anxious, she fell upon the breathing exercises taught to her during a round of cognitive behavioural treatment. It had seemed like a pampering session at the time, something she went to because her psychiatrist had recommended it, quite forcibly. Charlie had used it on occasion but found it less than fruitful. Until now.

She lowered her breasts; still aware they were completely exposed and stretched her neck, so her head fell back. The rain had eased off, her hooded lids now able to part so she could at least see a silhouette of her surroundings. The pain remained and the only thing that helped was the cold dirty water. Right now, she couldn't allow that to debilitate her.

Once she felt calmer, Charlie felt her way round the side wall of her prison. They felt damp, aged mildew slithering on to her trembling hands. One of the partitions had already fallen, a beam approximately half a meter in length and ten centimetres in width. At first it had seemed like nothing more than a loose piece of junk. Neither the wood, nor her captor had bargained for how resourceful Charlie could be. If she were going to die here, naked and alone she wasn't going down without a fight.

Charlie dug her nails into the side of where the broken partition used to be. There was plenty of space for her to grip it. Not wanting to break too little of it, she rocked it gently back and forth and listened until she was sure it had begun to crack. Moments later, Charlie triumphantly pulled a slat slightly longer and thicker than the piece she already had. She wanted to let out a cry of joy, the first reason she'd had today not to feel completely defeated. She muffled the sigh of relief that almost escaped because she didn't have the luxury of becoming complacent. Her attacker could return any minute. She could only imagine how angry he might be if he discovered what she was up to.

Another piece of wood came all too easily as she dug her nails in again. She continued with that very same process until she had broken off enough wood for her plan. Then she forced the tip of her fingers down into the depths of the mud, more determined this time and not just settling for a cupped hand of water.

Charlie began to burrow her fists until she was pulling away at the dirt. She didn't care that there might be creepy insects or worms in the gathering mounds, she only wanted to create a trench deep enough that it would house her body. Seconds felt like minutes, minutes felt like hours, but Charlie was long versed in the art of counting time. She'd lay awake enough nights, shaving off the horror of the nightmares a rapist had once gifted to her and now it came second nature to her.

Finally, after the longest time had passed, Charlie felt her way round her new space and wondered if it were deep enough for her to get into. She shuddered at what might approach her, but she shuddered more at the thought of her impending death. Her captor had his plan, she was forming hers. Climbing into the space, she felt along the edges to ensure it was just enough that she could move and breathe and that the upper cover wouldn't fall in on her.

Once she was certain it was safe, Charlie crawled back up into the dirt and wedged her wooden slats along the top of her trench. She threw back a matted strand of hair that was now tickling at her lips and took a deep breath. How much longer could she survive this?

She began to pull the mounds of surrounding dirt over the wooden slats, patting them as if she were making a round of pancakes. The thought of it made her feel hungry but that wasn't a worry for now. The main thing was that she managed to get out of the rain before it throttled down again. She would worry about the rest later.

Charlie continued to sweep the dirt across the

makeshift grave, ensuring there was only enough to cover it and not cave it in. Once she had completely covered her new haven, she brushed the rest of the dirt into a flat mound, blending it with the rest of her surroundings. She wasn't sure how it might look from above. What difference would it make anyway? If her captor returned and found her trickery, she'd probably be killed. She just hoped he used the same car that had woken her, the angry exhaust that had roared into the distance. There'd be no mistaking her captors return.

For now, she burrowed her way down into the new hole and finally remembered what it was like for the rain not to thunder down upon her aching skin.

29.

When Kate arrived at the refuge at just after nine a.m., she was feeling a little worse for wear. She had pulled her tousled hair back into a loose bun, threw on just enough makeup to conceal her raging hangover. 'I'm never drinking again,' she announced.

Natasha was at her desk, the expected mug of coffee steaming over a set of cards.

'Feeling a little tender, are we?'

'What's that you're doing?' Kate moved towards the desk, wondering if she were playing a game or if the cards were out for another reason.

'Tarot,' replied Natasha, absently. 'I dabble a little bit.'

'What are they saying?'

'Nothing I want to hear,' she said, packing them up and shuffling again.

'Guess who was at the restaurant last night?'

Natasha frowned, spinning her chair so that she was directly in front of Kate. 'Who?'

'Bloody Groundwater. Why does he seem to be everywhere I go these days?'

'He probably isn't. Why is he upsetting you so much?'

'Who said I'm upset?' Kate was getting a little irritable with everyone assuming she had some issue with Alan Groundwater.

Natasha stood, holding Kate firmly in her gaze. 'Your facial expression, your tone, your body language. Are you telling me I'm misreading it?'

Kate felt a little sheepish under the stare of someone as bold as Natasha. 'Maybe not. Don't you think it's strange though that he was here, then he turns up later in the same restaurant as me?'

'Didn't you go to a restaurant just around the corner from here?'

Kate nodded.

'Then why is it unthinkable that he'd turn up there. He'd not long left here with a flea in his ear, probably went to a bar to get hammered. I do have that effect on some men, you know?'

Kate laughed then. 'Not this one. He's too cock sure of himself. Even for you.'

'Don't be so sure. I've known Alan for a year or two. You're not the first student we've had here. Though you're the first one that hasn't been totally bowled over by his amazing sense of humour.'

'Amazing?' Kate wasn't sure whether to laugh or cry at that.

Natasha raised her eyebrows. 'That was my reaction as well. Seriously though, I had a girl in here who I thought was going to have a seizure one day.'

'Do you like him?'

'Yes,' replied Natasha. 'I don't think he's funny, nor do I think he's as clever as he thinks he is. But I think he's got a good heart. I really don't think he meant any harm coming here yesterday and you've got to not let it get to you.'

'He really embarrassed me. I thought you were going to march me out the door behind him.'

'He's involved in your learning. That means he'll be privy to some of what goes on in here. I don't like it because I'd rather keep information contained. The more people who know something, the less you're able to control it.'

Kate slumped a little in her chair, her head still pounding from the bottle of Chianti. 'You think I'm overthinking it?'

'I think when you don't like someone, you don't

have to look far to find their flaws.'

Kate looked back at the cards in Natasha's hand. 'Do you want to read me?'

She licked her lips. 'Okay but are you sure you're ready to learn what the cards are about to show you?' She laughed menacingly.

'I think I can hack it,' retorted Kate. 'By the way, Phil asked me to speak to you again about Michelle Evans. He just wanted to double check that she wasn't employed here. Would you mind having a look again?'

Natasha turned back to the laptop on her desk and pushed the tarot cards to the side. 'I guess your future can wait a few more minutes. As if we don't already know about your fairy-tale ending.'

Kate threw her head back, felt the room spin a little and wondered if she hadn't completely overreacted to a man who had done nothing but offer her help. Time to get a grip, she warned herself and waited to find out if Marina Cullen House really was the target of a madman.

30.

The earlier visit to Beth's childhood home hadn't been the fountain of information they had hoped. Marilyn Phinn had dived erratically between shock and bitterness, making her quite an unreliable source of information. Her refusal to enter Beth's bedroom had also proven problematic as they were unable to query many of the things they found. Ultimately, the biggest discovery they made was that there was nothing much to discover. At least they had the single loose hair to follow up on.

'I'm heading over to the GOC in a few minutes,' announced Phil as they forced past the dropping gale. The GOC was the main centre of operations for Glasgow's entire CCTV systems and the main place the police went when they needed access to any street camera footage.

'What is it you think you'll find?'

'Nothing,' replied Phil, knowing he sounded as frustrated as he felt. 'I want to look at the footage of Michelle's last documented moments and see if I can see anything else of interest. Maybe someone was nearby and would have seen her getting into a car or being forced off the street. Perhaps someone seen it and didn't think there was anything too untoward going on. Who knows? At this stage, we just need a break.'

'We really do. My concern is that the killer is already moving on to victim number three. There couldn't have been more than a day or two between discovering Michelle's body and Beth's disappearance.'

'That's true. Do you know what I was wondering about earlier on? Why didn't Marilyn Phinn report her daughter missing? I understand that Michelle's mother wouldn't have known as they live in separate countries and don't speak every day. Surely Marilyn must have noticed her daughter hadn't been home in a few days.' Phil tapped on the screen of his mobile phone, barely registering that Kate had tried to call him. 'Not that it matters now. I just hope we get a match for that hair.'

Donna nodded in agreement. 'Have we been able to find a list of all the parks that still have pits and shafts open to the public?'

'Not as easy as it sounds. It's just as well young Ryan Wilson broke his ankle. He's on desk duty, so I've got him on all the menial tasks that we don't have time to do ourselves. He's still compiling that list.'

Donna sighed. 'I'm still shocked that Marilyn had so little insight into her daughter's life. How can she not know something about her? Anything?'

Phil laughed and shook his head. 'Can you not remember being that age? Despite what people say, you're more defiant in your twenties than you are when you're thirteen. I lived with my folks well into adulthood and nothing irked me more than my mother asking me where I was going, who with and when I'd be back. I think I'd almost made detective before she stopped bothering to ask.'

'Always mummy's little boy.' Donna smiled. 'Anyway, do you think you'll be able to see anything on those grainy little videos over at GOC?'

'I don't think we'll see anything new. Right now, we've got very little. It's got to be worth a try. No point relying on Marilyn. She's wired up the wrong way.'

'She just lost her daughter,' Donna said.

'I know,' responded Phil, realising how harsh he must have sounded. 'I'm not trying to be unkind. I just wish she knew something that might have helped. She's an advert to all families out there to take more notice. Even when your family member is a single adult, pay attention. You don't know who the hell is lurking out there.'

~

The morning didn't transpire to be as long as they thought. On arriving at GOC, Phil discovered the manager, Mandy Brown had already downloaded a selection of video's round the time and area that they required.

Phil and Donna followed Mandy into a small square room devoid of atmosphere, housing a small table, two dinky chairs and a fired-up laptop. That was to be their office for the better part of the day, they realised as they plopped onto chairs.

'Right then, we better get started,' Phil said, edging past the first seat and lowering himself into the second. 'Can we get some water in here?'

'I'll ask Sandy to bring you some. He'll also do your tea and coffee if you need it. I don't know if you'll be here through lunch time, but he can also sort you out with sandwiches from the canteen.' Mandy was an older woman, a broad Glasgow accent, her hair teased into curls that probably should have been cut out ten years ago. Her face was too brown to be a natural tan in the current January climate whilst every feature on her face spread into a selection of well-worn lines. She seemed friendly enough, if not a little on edge by their presence.

'You get lunch here? I think I'll come here to work.'

Mandy smiled. 'You're out of luck. We've just

let some staff go. Anyway, who'll keep the streets safe if we have you lot transferring over here?' She brushed at her shoulder and smirked. 'Besides, the food really isn't *that* good.'

Phil swore under his breath as the first of the videos, dated twelfth of January, began to play. He forwarded through hours of grainy footage until the time he knew his first victim would appear. Just as he knew she would, Michelle Evans emerged from the distance, her head tucked under a hood, her arms across her breasts as she warded off the wind. He watched as she disappeared into the pharmacy, the details of which were documented on another grainy video that they'd managed to obtain from the store security.

Donna sat beside him on a different screen, watching a different place and time. Linn Park, the place where Michelle had taken her final breath. 'What am I looking for here?'

Phil watched Michelle re-appear at the door of the pharmacy and re-cover her head. 'There's no footage of anyone carrying a body in. Which means they would have to drive in, then drive out again.'

'What if they didn't use any of the gates?'

He shrugged. 'Then they would have to have thrown the body over a fence somewhere in the vicinity of the park. There's no other sign of injury or violence on Michelle's body. She was carefully taken to the place of her death and gently lowered into that pit.'

'I'm looking for a car then?'

'Exactly.'

'Look at the amount of people coming and going in these tapes. How could a killer get a girl into that park with all those prying eyes?'

‘Don’t forget how secluded that little pocket of the park is. Barely anybody even knows it exists, other than the caretaker. The killer must have known that as well. Maybe he drove in during the day but waited until after dark to do his worst.’

Donna reached for her pen and pad. ‘It’s a long time to keep someone quiet. There wasn’t that much sedative in her blood.’

‘There’s a lot of things that don’t make sense. There’s no sign of ligatures round the wrists or ankles. No indication of a gag over their mouth. I’m wondering the same thing as you. How do you take someone into a public place, presumably awake and free to move and scream, but not have them kick up a stink?’

Silently, Donna started to scribble on the notepad, taking down the registration, make and colour of every car that came and went from the park. ‘Do you know what strikes me here?’ She jabbed her finger at the screen. ‘Lots of people. Wasn’t it later that day the weather really took a turn for the worse?’

‘They’re probably just taking advantage of the last decent day we got. The videos from the next day will tell a different story.’ He clicked off the screen and searched for the next video which would only confirm there were no more sightings of Michelle from the time she left the pharmacy, which left him increasingly frustrated. They had assumed she was taken immediately after. For all Phil knew, she might well have shopped, went for drinks, attended church and a concert before falling prey to her attacker.

Donna groaned then. ‘The killer must have known the only camera’s covering Linn Park was at the gates. Is that public knowledge?’

‘You can find out anything from the bloody

internet. It's not like when we were starting out. It was easier to narrow things down then. Now, you could be looking at anybody with an internet connection.'

'And there were no tyre marks at all?'

'Nothing. That's the biggest conundrum of all. Particularly with Beth Phinn when the ground was much worse. How did he get her from the car to the pit without leaving a single trace of himself or his vehicle? Also, how does a person carry someone else without leaving a single fibre of clothing or DNA on them?'

'Don't forget the hair found on Beth's head,' corrected Donna.

'I know, we're still waiting on an identity. Why does everything take so bloody long?' Another file clicked on, Phil looked up to find a tray with two glasses and a jug of water. 'Christ, they've even chopped up some lemon.'

The young delivery man smiled modestly. 'We aim to please.'

For the next few hours, as Donna continued to search footage from the next few days, Phil began to cross reference all the cars that came and went through those gates.

Eventually, Donna grew exasperated. 'This is worse than Sudoku and you know how much I hate that.' She tucked her hair behind her ears and threw herself back in the chair.

It was then that Mandy Brown re-appeared in the doorway. 'Any luck?'

Outside, thunder and lightning exploded across the skies in perfect harmony.

Phil leapt to his feet. 'My arms and legs are killing me from sitting here, my eyes are starting to spin and it's like a furnace in here. And no, we've still not found anything that will lead us to the killer. Several of these cars make repeat journeys to the park. Many of them will be dog walkers or fitness fanatics.'

'Who the hell jogs in this weather? Or takes their poor pet out in it? Someone should phone the NSPCC.' Mandy delivered her summation without any change to her tone, which made Phil snicker slightly.

Donna returned to the screen. 'I'm now on the tapes from outside Jordanhill Park. I swear these registration numbers are all starting to look the same.'

Mandy squinted at her. 'I'll let you get back to it then. Remember, we close the office at six.'

Phil didn't know if he had the stamina to be there until six. He was already square eyed from staring at the grey screen for too long.

Beside him, Donna continued to scribble on the notepad. Approximately half an hour later, she let out a loud gasp.

Phil was startled, realising he was about to drift off. 'What?' He darted forward in his seat.

'Bingo!'

He rolled his seat over to her and tightened his eyes. 'What am I seeing here?'

Donna ran her pen aggressively across the page, underscoring a registration number that had already been written several times. 'Three visits to Linn Park, now I've got the car going into Jordanhill Park. It's the same car, Phil.'

He paused the video and stared at the old green Volkswagen, now sailing past the gates and heading towards the back end of the park. A ladder was thrown onto the top and tied haphazardly so that it was almost sliding off. 'Get Ryan, or Steve to run the registration plate. Tell them it's a priority.'

Donna rose from the desk and clapped her hands, excitedly.

'I want the owner of that car brought in for questioning before they have a chance to do anything to anyone else.' Phil turned back to the frozen image on the screen and drew a large breath in. Finally, they had a real lead.

31.

As he opened his eyes, the sound of the weatherman on television announcing a red weather warning, Garry felt his head thud from the arrival of his own storm; a raging hangover. Why do it to himself, he wondered for the hundredth time in his life?

He sat up, reached for his cigarettes and rubbed the bridge of his nose with his index finger and thumb. He gasped, remembering the state his face had been left in after last night's brawl. Still in yesterday's clothes, he headed for the back garden for his morning smoke. Or was it afternoon?

A momentary slither of sunlight broke through the tumbling of clouds, creating the illusion it was brighter than it really was. As Garry stepped into the back court, he realised just how cold it was. He lit the end of the cigarette and blew a hue of purple smoke around himself.

A few minutes later he headed back into the flat, deciding that he needed to text or call his sister before she arrived home. Garry wasn't good with words, which had always been an issue in any relationship he'd been in. It didn't matter with Charlie though. She'd be happy to know he was safe and that he was sorry for giving her crap the night before.

Garry's plan for today was simple. He'd contact Charlie, let her know what had happened, offer to take her for dinner and all would be good. He'd then arrange to meet that scumbag Tony, give him a jab for disappearing last night before hitting the town for another night of hard drinking and skirt chasing. He particularly relished getting on the spirits to numb the pain of his cracked ribs.

He hit the send button on his apology text then

heard Charlie's phone resound back from her bedroom. She'd gone to work without her phone? She rarely had the thing out of her hand. How strange that she'd go without it. Perhaps she was home?

Garry noticed the bedroom door was slightly ajar, but he knocked anyway. With no response, he pushed his way into the room, noticing that her clothes from the night before were strewn across the bed. A slim line of sunlight broke through the drape of turquoise voile and landed a flush of blue and purple on a silver lamp.

Another beep from the phone, this time a message from someone else. He slowly reached for the phone, which lay squarely on the centre of the duvet.

A message from someone called Natasha appeared above his most recent one.

'Hi, hope you're okay, Charlie. Can you phone in and let me know you're okay. I've had to mark you off sick, but I'm just concerned…'

The rest of the message could only be accessed by unlocking the phone, something Garry wouldn't do unless necessary. Besides, he didn't know Charlie's code. He lifted his eyes to see the ghost of a naked tree waving in the wind outside the window. Then he turned to scour the room in case she was injured. 'Charlie?'

He moved towards her bathroom, gripping her phone in his sweating hand. He wouldn't allow himself to think the worst. Not yet. There must be a reasonable explanation. Perhaps she'd been so angry by their exchange last night that she'd decided to have a day off from the world. He'd had those days himself.

A step into the bathroom revealed all he needed

to know to confirm that his sister hadn't just gone off on her own. Her towel was strewn along the lining of the bath. As he leaned down onto the floor, he could see a tiny speck of blood on the white tiles. It was small, but enough to raise his concern. Then he saw the sink, a mug smashed onto the ceramic and a slightly open penknife that he recognised.

'I gave you this,' he said, as he reached down and touched it. He remembered the moment too well. It was before Charlie had ventured back into the real world, a time where she was still afraid of her own shadow. He'd encouraged her to take baby steps out of the family home because he feared if she didn't do it soon, she'd never leave again. It was one of the token gifts he had delivered along with a session of self-defence with one of his army buddies and a host of advice on how to survive the crippling effects of PTSD.

Garry stared at the window again. His entire body now felt drenched from the glut of sweat. He didn't have time to panic now. Nor did he have time to pity himself. He had to find Charlie. The only place he could turn was the unit she worked at. He knew little about her working life, only that it was a refuge for abused women.

Quietly and without fuss, he headed to the lounge, placing Charlie's penknife into his pocket. If that monster had been released and had come for his sister, there would be no stopping Garry this time. His parents had once held him back from committing the act of murder. There wouldn't be a second reprieve for Johnny McCabe. If McCabe had put a single finger on Charlie, he would be a dead man.

32.

Phil stood at the end of the corridor and stared earnestly out of the window. It seemed like eternity since the sky had darkened to this opaque grey and nobody seemed able to say when it would lighten again. With the gloom of the day came the dip in his mood. These new bleak surroundings didn't help either. Gone was the camaraderie he and his colleagues shared before they were all farmed into this new larger head office. He longed for a familiar face to step out from inside one of the rooms. Nobody did, so he turned and walked to his destination.

'Did you manage to find out what I asked you?'

Ryan looked younger than he was, particularly when he was sitting down. When the boy stood, he towered over everyone else in the building. Sat down, with dishevelled blonde hair, smooth chin and squinty tie, he could have passed for someone of school age. 'There was nothing really to find out. Groundwater is as clean as a brand-new whistle. Christ, he even gives free tuition to learning disabled people in the local community. I don't think we can say much more than that.'

'I suspected that would be the case.'

'Why are you looking into him? Does he have something to do with the star murders?'

Phil waved his hand. 'If only. It would please Kate if I could pin something on him. She's taken a real dislike to him.'

'Oh dear. If she's anything like my Missus, there'll be no moving her on the subject. If Lucy takes a dislike to someone, they better duck for cover.'

'It's not like Kate to take such a dislike to

someone. Anyway, thanks for looking. What about the registration I gave you?'

'That was even easier,' boasted Ryan. 'It belongs to a Kenneth Black. I've got the address here for you.'

Phil snatched it lightly and smirked. 'Blackwood Farm in Thorntonhall.'

'It's in your stomping ground. Somewhere between Glasgow and East Kilbride. I've never been myself, but I think it's rural enough that someone could easily live out there and not be on the radar.'

'Do you know exactly where it is?'

'I've google mapped it, had a look at the street view. Last notable image shows it to be quite dilapidated and I couldn't find anything online to suggest it's a working farm.'

'Anything on Mr. Black?'

'Numerous domestic incidents back in the nineties. As far as I can tell, he has kept a low profile since.' Ryan loaded the image of the farmhouse on to the screen and pushed his chair out of the way. 'The Volkswagen is ancient. You normally get fifteen to twenty years out of a car, max. This one is nearly twenty-five years old. Do you honestly think this old guy, in his late fifties is running around in an ancient car and kidnapping women?'

'He's not exactly straining himself. He debilitates them by spraying acid in their eyes, then knocks them out with tranquilizer before bundling them into his car. From the little evidence we do have, it doesn't look like he has much contact with them until after they're dead.'

Ryan lurched forward. 'He'd still have to have some strength though.'

Phil was about to argue that some of the most

heinous crimes had been carried out by slobs when his phone rang. 'Excuse me, I need to get this,' he explained, noticing Kate calling him for the third time this morning. He stepped out of the office.

Kate's voice sounded panicked, breathless even. 'Phil, Charlie hasn't turned up for work this morning. Her brother has just phoned to say that her flat has been messed up and that there's been a disturbance in her bathroom.'

'What kind of disturbance?' He gave Ryan a quick wave and then began the short journey back to the second floor.

'He says there was blood on her bathroom floor and her mobile phone had been left on her bed. He says she never goes anywhere without it. He said it's not the first time she's been attacked and then mumbled something about killing the guy who is tormenting her. I think Natasha is also really worried in light of everything that has happened.'

'Have you managed to find anything on Michelle Evans? Has she ever worked there?'

'Nothing. Natasha had a look again today, right before she told me I'd be an old spinster and that I'd be travelling alone soon.'

'Eh?'

'I'll tell you later. Anyway, about Charlie. What are we going to do?'

'I'll get someone over to her flat to have a look but there's no reason to get upset yet, Kate. People cut themselves in the bathroom all the time and if we looked into every untidy bedroom and forgotten phone-,' Phil eyed the horizon, focusing on an old abandoned church that spired into the crashing clouds. For now, the thunder lay dormant, but he still felt dread coat his gut. 'Can you give me her brother's phone number so I can try and get in touch with him?'

'I'll text it to you,' she offered, ending the call.

Phil returned to Ryan and lowered himself back into a chair, unknotting his tie. 'You'd never know it was minus five outside. I am sweating like a pig in muck.'

'You look harassed mate. Everything okay?'

Phil popped the phone back onto the table and threw his head back. 'One of Kate's workmates hasn't turned up. Her brother is staying with her now and he's found her bathroom a bit messed up.

'Are you going to check it out?'

'I said I would. Meanwhile, I'm more interested in what Mr Black has to say.'

'You think he's your culprit?'

Phil sighed loudly. 'Right now, he's the best lead I've got.'

33.

Now that she had time to be terrified, Charlie had imagined every possible outcome. As she cowered under the darkness of her makeshift roof, she feared she might be buried alive. If the storm really took hold, the chances were some of the rotted wood might fall away from the edge of the rotunda and an avalanche of dirt might fall upon her. There were the other scenarios that her paranoid mind has begun to fashion, but nothing as grim as being buried alive. Still, her ears raised up every now and then, listening for the arrival of the roaring engine that had dumped her here.

The worst thing about lying in the darkness, surrounded by her thoughts of death was that it also opened her mind to him. She dared not say his name, but it didn't distract her from thinking about him. He was always there, not always at the forefront but always lingering and refusing to ever fully leave.

Charlie didn't fully remember her latest attack. Her last memory was of feeling in danger, something lurking in her bathroom as she took off her clothes. She had made it very easy for him to attack her, she realised. Now she berated herself once more because she had armed herself with the physical and mental tools, but she hadn't utilised them when it mattered most. She realised now how ill-judged her arrogance had been. She hadn't been the match she hoped she would be. Just the same old feeble person she'd been all that time ago when *he* had broken into her house, raped and dug a blade into her chest.

Other thoughts came and went, caught between thoughts that comforted her. Charlie thought of her parents, probably now enjoying their time on a beach far from her plight. It almost made her happy to know they would be completely unaware of the situation she was in. A slight smile, cracking through the pain and she dared to swallow back her tears before they stung her burning eyes. Her thoughts turned then to Garry. She suddenly felt a tinge of hope. Garry? He was staying with her which meant that he would notice she was missing. She once feared that her brother would tear off someone's head for her. Now she prayed for it.

A song popped into her head, a melancholy tune with no vocals. It was her peace song, the one she used to listen to on her phone when she couldn't sleep. She'd turn it up just loud enough that it would drown out the battles in her head but keep her alert to the outside world. It tinkled in her mind, soothing her like chimes of comfort. The thought of her parents, smiling and re-assuring, the song that had eased her into a gentle slumber many nights and the ferocity of a big brother who would never give up on her was enough to make her grasp for hope. Maybe she wouldn't die here today. Though, for the briefest moment when she was at her worst, Charlie could almost wish that death would rush along and take her. A thought she hoped she'd never know again. She turned her head, staring at the little gape of light above her and felt lucky she'd found a way to save herself. At least for now.

34.

It wasn't nearly as difficult to watch them taking their last breath as he had imagined. He had loomed over them, like the shadow of death waiting for them to die. If he needed any consoling, which wasn't very likely, it was that he hadn't physically drained the life from them himself. In his mind, he knew he had never physically taken anyone's life. One day, if he should ever have a sudden pang of conscience, he might remind himself of that. Not now! Now, he was savouring the power.

He hid in a dark room at the end of a corridor, caressing his crotch because the excitement of this new power made him hard. It had never been about sex. That didn't mean he couldn't enjoy the moment.

Once again, he reminded himself he hadn't chosen his victims because of any physical attraction. It had helped that they were pretty. That they were pretty and had been attracted to him only made it easier. Once they moved beyond the initial flirtation, he would begin to feel irritable of them and that only made torturing them more pleasurable.

He unzipped his trousers and slipped his hand inside.

The thought of his latest victim was the most delicious yet. Charlie Westmore. He imagined her squirming in agony as worms crawled across her hands and feet, screaming as those little juicy beasts feasted on a hundred tiny blood spots.

Right now, victim three would be experiencing what he once experienced, the horrifying fear of wondering when someone would come and save her. He traced the line of his face with a single finger and blew into the air. In his vision, he caught sight of a tiny clearing in the sky, the speckle of stars twinkling at him and it reminded him why he was doing this in the first place.

He suddenly stopped pleasuring himself, the realisation that she would be watching him from afar, scolding silently from the sky. A momentary crash to earth, the clarity right before ejaculation and he suddenly slapped himself. Anger took over. The anger that drove him and led him to become a killer. He felt overwhelmed, the amazement that he was already more than halfway through his work. Two and a half lives down. Only one more to snatch. All of them innocent in their own little way, all paying the price for something that happened to a little boy a very long time ago.

35.

'You can't be in here,' screeched an unfamiliar voice.

Kate spun round, nearly spilling the contents of the bowl on her lap in the process. She could see a man pushing his way into the hall and shoving the much smaller woman aside.

'Hey, you can't do that.' The woman was pulling at his arm now.

Kate, feeling a surge of panic, watched Natasha emerge from the office.

'Can I help you?'

'I want to see my sister,' he shouted, staggering past the woman who had been the first barricade.

'Your sister?'

'Charlie,' he shouted. 'She's not at home and this is the only other place I know that she comes.'

Natasha lifted her arms to calm him. 'Charlie isn't here, sweetheart. I have sent her a message because I'm concerned about her, but she hasn't shown up today.' Her voice was soothing but firm at the same time.

He snarled. 'Something's happened to her. She doesn't just not turn up. That's not who she is. Even before everything,' his voice trailed off and his eyebrows dipped, as if he were recalling a painful memory.

Kate, realising he must be the brother Charlie had been talking about, remembered she had spoken to him earlier on the phone. He'd sounded calm then, a little tetchy but still in the wings of sobriety. She had relayed Garry's concerns to Phil who had asked her to obtain a phone number next time he called. Kate had expected, or at least hoped she wouldn't have to hear from him again because hearing from him meant that something may just have happened to Charlie after all. The thought sent a shiver down Kate's spine.

'Have you called the police?'

'No,' he hissed.

'Well, isn't that the first thing you should have done?' Natasha retained the same composure that she had in all situations, yet she was firm enough that it seemed Garry was already calming. 'Maybe it would be better for you to go and do that. Leave it to the professionals.'

He stopped swaying, leaned against a post and appeared to consider what she was saying.

Kate wondered why he hadn't called the police. He was concerned something happened to his sister so shouldn't they have been the first number on his dial pad.

'What's your name, sweetheart?'

Garry looked up and blinked his watering eyes. 'Garry Shanks.'

'Well, look. It isn't appropriate for you to be in here, Garry. This is a safe space for women and children who are already vulnerable. You understand that I need to put them first, don't you?' If Natasha felt at all threatened or shaken by Garry's intrusion, she was too steely to show it. She moved towards him, resting a hand on his forearm, turning him back towards the door.

He suddenly spun away from her. 'I want to speak to the woman who answered the phone to me earlier.'

Kate edged one step forward, her gut tumbling into itself and held up her hand. 'That was me. I spoke to you earlier.'

Natasha held up her hand. 'Its fine, Kate. I've got this under control. Garry is going to go outside and call the police. Once he's filed a report, we'll be only too happy to help in any way we can. Right now, all these people are waiting for him to leave.'

Kate's gaze traced the direction of Natasha's hand and she found the gauntlet of angry, frightened faces lining up the hall behind her. 'I need your phone number, Garry. My partner needs to speak to you. He'll help you find Charlie.'

He guffawed. 'Help me find her? If that rapist has taken her, we've no chance of finding her. He failed the first time. Do you think he's going to risk prison a second time?'

'Rapist?' Kate was confused. Since learning that Charlie hadn't turned in for work, Kate had tried to bury the thought that she might have fallen foul of the killer that Phil was working to find. He had never mentioned anything about rape.

Natasha peered over her shoulder at Kate. 'If something has happened to her, we need to let the police deal with it. This,' she lifted a pointed finger and jabbed it at Garry's shoulder, 'isn't the way to deal with it. You're frightening my residents.'

'I'm sorry,' was all he could muster.

'Look, I'm still on my break. There's a café two doors along. Let's go there and wait while I try to speak to Phil.' Kate followed him to the door, trying to ignore the pungent stench of alcohol.

'That sounds wise,' offered Natasha, letting her guard down just enough to look flustered. 'Come on girls, let's get the kids back to the playroom and get you all calmed down.'

Kate smiled, thankful that Natasha didn't make an issue of her offer. She didn't feel frightened of Garry, despite his aggressive stance when he appeared at the refuge door. She was more frightened of what might have happened to Charlie. Now that the mention of a rapist had been thrown into the mix, Kate had a growing sense of despair. She sensed Garry wasn't aware that the two previous murders could be related to the refuge. In fact, Kate suspected Garry was talking about someone else. Something had happened to Charlie before. Which meant that there could be a double threat to Charlie's life. Kate buried the thought and followed him to the nearby cafe. There, she would learn exactly what it was Charlie had endured that had forced her to change her identity and flee her hometown.

36.

Phil had found himself snoozing in the chair as he eyeballed the extensive report on Kenneth Black's arrests. Three for drunken disorderly, two domestic assaults and several others for fighting. All the arrests involved his late wife, or brawls in the local pub. There was nothing that stood out to suggest this man could suddenly devise such a plan to murder two women. Not to mention the twenty-year time frame since his last arrest.

'We've got a name, Steve,' announced Phil as he watched his younger colleague saunter into the room. 'Kenneth Black.'

A smile spread across Steve's narrow face as he dropped into his chair and swung like an impatient schoolboy. 'Let's get him arrested then.'

'Hang fire, cannonball. We're not shooting over to arrest him in the next ten minutes. These things take time, precision and patience. We've got to build a case and present it so we can get a warrant. We have his car in both places several times over the days where Michelle and Beth were dumped. We don't have a motive or even a connection between this man and the girls.'

Steve, suitably scolded, threw his hands up. 'Any previous convictions?'

'Several arrests for violence, including several domestic incidents. Though, his wife decided not to press charges. Back then, the onus was on the victim to bring charges, and prove it was domestic abuse. Nowadays, they want to throw away the key.'

Steve scowled. 'The way it should always have been.'

'There's also the location,' said Phil, redirecting

the conversation slightly. 'This man owns a hundred acres of land. Why would he need to take the bodies anywhere else? He could dump them on his own land and they'd probably not be found for years.'

'I think he wants them to be found though.'

'I'm just saying that if he wanted them to die, there's no need to go taking them to public parks,' interrupted Phil.

Donna perched herself at the end of the pod of tables and shrugged. 'I'd be more concerned if this made sense to you. At the end of the day, however clever he fancies himself, he's just a nutter killing innocent women to make himself feel more of a man.'

'If a man had said that about a woman, you'd accuse him of being a misogynist,' grumbled Steve.

'Okay, you two,' said Phil, once again the referee at a match he didn't really want to be at. 'Let's cut the crap and get out of here. I want my streets safe again. We've already had over a hundred calls this morning from people in a panic because they saw someone lurking at their door, or in their garden, or on their street corner. Let's find out exactly what Mr. Black knows.'

~

'I'm just going to ask, is there something wrong with you recently?'

Donna gulped back the words for fear that if she started to rant, she might never stop. 'Why?'

'You must have noticed you haven't been yourself. You're short with everybody, we've invited you for dinner twice and you've cancelled it at the last minute and, quite frankly, you've been a first-class pain in the backside.'

'Charming,' she hissed.

'Look, I'm not asking you for the reason you

think I am,' he said, turning on the ignition to prepare for the drive to Thorntonhall. 'I honestly don't give a crap that you don't like Steve, though it is becoming wearisome hearing about it. That's a non-issue right now. I can see that something is getting to you and I really want to help. So, you can either tell me to mind my own business or you can remember how long we've been partners and friends.'

Donna bit on her lip, contemplating the reality of saying it out loud. Up until now she had been able to bury herself in work, though she was very aware that she must be getting on everyone's nerves. She was getting on her own.

'What is it he's done that bothers you so much?'

She pushed down the urge to cry. Then she silently scolded herself. Why couldn't she just cry in front of Phil of all people? It's not like she'd never broken down in front of him before.

Phil was leaning in on her now, his faded reflection dark in the rain-soaked window. 'If you can't speak to me, call over and see Kate. If it's something I can't help with, maybe you'll feel more comfortable with her.'

Truth was, Donna didn't feel any more or less comfortable with Kate than she did with Phil. They were both her friends, so much so she had come to know them as a singular entity, rather than the two individuals they may once have been. 'It's not that,' she finally said. 'My mum has to go into a nursing home. She's too far gone, and I can't take care of her any longer.' Before she'd even said the last word, she lost the battle for composure and began to wail.

Phil rushed towards her and threw his arm round her shoulders. 'Bloody crap, no wonder you've been out of sorts. Why didn't you say anything?'

Donna could taste the salt of her tears as she ran her hand across her nose. 'It's been getting worse for months. It started with small things at first, strange conversations about things that happened when I was little. Then last month, she nearly burned down my kitchen. You remember that day I called in sick, that was why. I'm now having to farm my kids out to relatives and neighbours to make my shifts. Even that's becoming more and more of a struggle. My next-door neighbour goes in and puts out her meals while I'm at work and checks that she's safe.' She took a deep breath and turned to face him. Her eyes felt swollen red; her face exhausted but she could finally feel her shoulders relax for the first time in weeks. 'I made the decision a few days ago. My day off last week was spent going around places to find somewhere that could cater for her needs.'

'That must have been a difficult decision to make,' he said, reassuringly. He continued to run his hand up and down the arch in her back.

'Don't be kind to me. I can take just about anything else today, but if you're kind to me I'll probably go completely to bits.'

'You could have told me. That's what I'm here for. I might even have cut you a break over this Steve nonsense.'

She laughed, realising how awful she must have seemed. Not that she thought she and Steve would be bosom buddies very soon but perhaps her own issues had made her shorter than she would normally be. Perhaps she would apologise later. Only if it didn't stick in her craw.

'Listen, if you need any help with childcare, Kate and I can help if we're on different days. They're a great distraction for Harry anyway.'

'Wait until Kate finds out you've volunteered her,' laughed Donna, her lips finally still enough to arch into a smile.

'She won't be pleased you've struggled on and not asked for help. For Christ sake, don't let this happen again,' he scolded.

'I won't.'

He squeezed her shoulder and gave her his most reassuring smile. 'We'll work it out, together.' With that, he slammed his foot down on the clutch and pulled out of the car park.

37.

The farmhouse was every bit as wild as it had been in the street view image that Ryan had shown Phil. In fact, as he turned to face another pounding of thunder, Phil wondered how the wooden house had ever withstood a storm half as bad as this. As he climbed onto the charcoal porch and knocked on the door, Phil eyed the front of the house for any signs of a car. There were none. The only tyre tracks he could see were the ones he and Donna had just made.

The land itself seemed as if it had been a long time since it produced. There were no animals as Phil might have expected to find on a farm. The crops were long dead, the trees barren and the only source of any natural energy being a single wind turbine near the centre of the land. The whole land seemed at odds with the beauty of the natural outdoors.

'Who is it?' The drone of a drunk called from inside.

Phil held up his identity card to a small glass window just above eye level. 'Police Scotland. My name's Detective Inspector Phil Morris. I need to speak to you about your car.'

'My car?' roared the voice from inside, the door creaking open, so his twitching eye was only just visible. 'What about it?'

'Can we come in?'

'No,' he answered, pulling the door slightly more so that he was now revealing his lined face under a bundle of wild white hair. When he smirked at Donna, he revealed a row of jagged yellow teeth, some of which looked like they hadn't been brushed or treated in a decade.

'Mister Black, we don't want this to be

unpleasant. We just have a few questions about your whereabouts on the twelfth and nineteenth of January. I'm sure you know about the storm. I don't really want any of us to be standing out here in the cold.'

He looked at them both pensively, focusing more on Donna but his eyes darting furiously between them. He seemed to be having an inner fight with himself because he repeatedly smacked his tongue against the roof of his mouth, tusking and muttering before finally opening the door to reveal the inner shadows of the hallway.

Donna was the first to touch the tip of her nose, as if protecting her nostrils from whatever unseemly scent was about to crawl up them.

Phil scanned the dreary surroundings and eyed an assortment of ancient junk stored in a pile at the end of the hall. He also noted the broken stairs and the snapped beams supporting the bannister and wondered how often they were used. In his assessment of the place, Kenneth Black was living in a death trap waiting to happen.

'I never go over the door. I don't even use a car.'

'You don't have a car?' Donna followed him into the lounge, a large square room that was surprisingly more modern and tidier than the rest of the bleak surroundings.

'Did I say I didn't own a car?' There was a constant brittleness in Kenneth's tone, and a certain mistrust that hung heavy in the atmosphere.

Phil stepped out from behind her. He was also surprised to find the lounge was most habitable. A modern flat screen hung on the back wall, leaning over a white oval fireplace and perfectly framed for the man to treat his arched leather sofa like a day at the cinema. 'So, what you're telling us is that you do own a car, but you don't use it.'

'I'm telling you nothing,' said Kenneth, hostility dripping from every word.

Phil caught a glimpse of a barn, equally torn looking and saw that the door was flapping in the wind. 'Is that where you keep it?'

'No!'

'Mister Black, why were you in Glasgow on the twelfth and nineteenth of January?'

'I wasn't,' he replied, defiantly, reaching for a bottle of whiskey and smacking the neck against the rim of a glass. 'Care for a drink?' Then he let out a throaty laugh to a joke that nobody else was being welcomed into.

'I'm driving,' said Phil. 'How much of that do you go through in a day?'

The man slammed the bottle down, lifted his head slowly and snarled. 'What the fuck has it got to do with you? How much do you drink every day?'

'Do you drink before you drive?'

'No,' Kenneth said.

'You don't think it's possible you've went somewhere when you've been drunk and forgotten?' Phil didn't think it was very likely. Seeing the life Kenneth Black led, his arthritic hands and how unmeasured his behaviour was, Phil had already made the assertion they might be barking up the wrong tree. Still, there was the car to explain.

'I think I'd have remembered driving to Glasgow.' Another throaty laugh, this time paired with a sarcastic echo.

'Does anyone else use your car?'

'Don't think so.'

'It would help if you were able to tell us where it is now. Your co-operation would be welcome, saves us the time of having to get a warrant and you the hassle of police going through your personal things.'

'Are you threatening me?' Kenneth slammed his glass on the same table he previously rested the bottle on. 'You don't have any reason to get a warrant. I've done nothing. What the hell's this about anyhow?'

'We're investigating the death of two young women who were found near where your car was seen.'

'My Volkswagen?' The colour appeared to drain from his already grey face.

Phil moved across the room, taking advantage of the heat that blared from the fire. When he looked at Donna, he could see she was still struggling with the questionable aroma. 'That's the one.'

'Couldn't have been my car. I told you, I don't use it.'

'Then who is using it?' Donna began to scribble some notes on a small notepad.

'Nobody,' he replied, keeping his eyes dipped.

Phil could pick a liar from a line-up of a hundred and Kenneth Black wasn't even a good one. 'Do you know either of these girls?' He held up a photo each of Michelle Evans and Beth Phinn.

'No,' said Kenneth, wrapping a trembling hand round his glass.

'You've never seen them before.'

Kenneth suddenly lost his temper, climbed to his feet and stormed to the lounge door. 'What is this? I barely leave the house. I don't use the bloody car. I've never seen those women before in my life.'

Phil was caught agape by the sudden outburst.

'I want you both to leave. Feel free to waste your time getting a warrant. I've got nothing to hide and you're not getting my permission to be going through my things.'

Phil ushered for Donna to go first, noting her relief that she was finally getting out of there. 'It would be easier if you just told us where the car is or who you've given it to. Would save us having to come back with a warrant. I'm a decent guy for a copper. Whoever turns up with the warrant to go through your stuff might not be so decent.'

'You should be strung up, you lot,' hissed Kenneth. 'Threatening an elderly vulnerable man.'

Phil wanted to laugh in Kenneth's face. There was nothing vulnerable about him. Phil imagined that a rattle snake would come off worse in a battle with Kenneth. 'I'm sure they'll take that into consideration,' he said, smirking. He followed Donna onto the porch.

'Do you believe him?' Donna took in a lungful of cold fresh air as the door slammed behind them.

'I don't think he's fit for the murders. That's not to say he's not helping someone. What's the fuss about the car all about?'

'If he's given it to someone and they've used it to commit murder, he's probably crapping himself.'

'Nah, if someone borrows your car and it's then associated with a murder, you would be tripping over yourself to put some distance between you and them as quickly as possible,' said Phil, looking back and noticing that Kenneth Black was standing behind a curtain. 'He's watching us.'

Donna turned her head and gave him a gentle smile. 'You think he knows anything about it?'

'I think he knows something he's not telling us. I don't think he's protecting someone. I think he's frightened of someone, and he doesn't trust us.'

'What can we do?'

Phil rubbed his hands together, warding off a stiff wind. 'What we told him we were going to do. Get a warrant. There's no better persuasion. He must make a choice now between trusting us and leaving his life in the hands of whoever is responsible for the murders. I think he already knows if he sticks with the killer, he's unlikely to come out of this alive.'

38.

As he wrung his fringe out with his hands, Garry looked as if he might explode.

'You said something about a rapist?'

He shook his head. 'I shouldn't have said anything. She's always telling me I need to learn to keep my temper under control.'

Kate took a sip of her diet coke and nudged her head in his direction. 'What happened?'

'This old thing?' He held his hands at the side of his battered face, revealing his knuckles were just as bruised. 'I had the old face for thirty years. I fancied a change.'

She chuckled. 'Bit of an extreme makeover.'

He nodded. 'You're Charlie's friend?'

'Not really,' admitted Kate, wondering why she'd been so concerned by someone she'd known for less than a week. 'I only met her earlier this week when I started volunteering at the refuge. I really like her though.'

'She's easy to like, my sister. Not like me. I'd create a riot in an empty room, as you can see.'

'I'm sure that's not true,' said Kate, shifting on the edge of the seat. 'Charlie was very excited to see you. It's all she talked about yesterday.'

'Until I pissed her off last night.'

'She won't care about that. And right now, the only important thing is finding out she's safe.'

He clenched his jaw and drew his eyes around the place, as if he expected to get to the bottom of it by leering at everybody else in the café.

'My fiancé is a policeman. I've called him and told him about her bathroom. He wants to speak to you.'

‘So, you think something’s happened to her as well?’

Kate suddenly felt apprehensive. Should she mention Phil’s investigation? It had been all over the news. Though she didn’t want to cause another flare up of Garry’s temper. ‘I don’t know. Just that Natasha said it’s not like her to not show up.’

‘Nah, there’s something else. I can read it in your face. What are you not saying?’

She flushed, rubbing her right wrist rigidly. ‘Nothing. I promise you. Phil just wants what we want, to know that she’s safe. That’s why he wants you to call him, or for me to pass on your number.’

He shrugged. ‘My experience with the police is that they’re not very helpful. We practically had to hand them Johnny McCabe on a platter. He’d still be walking the streets if we hadn’t led them to him.’

‘Johnny McCabe?’

He eyed her suspiciously. ‘She hasn’t mentioned any of this?’

Kate shook her head. ‘As I said, I’ve only known her a few days. Perhaps she didn’t feel comfortable sharing something personal with me.’ Even though Kate hadn’t previously known about Charlie’s rape and Garry hadn’t said McCabe was the rapist, it didn’t take much to join the dots.

‘So, you think he can help?’

‘Maybe. Do you want to file a missing person report?’

'Doesn't she have to be missing for twenty-four hours before I can do that?'

Kate wasn't sure. 'You seem panicked. You also seem like a guy who doesn’t usually panic. If you believe something has happened to her, you should definitely contact the police and file a report officially.'

He didn't seem convinced.

'What's the worst that can happen? She turns up and gets annoyed that you made a fuss. The worst-case scenario is much worse than that, isn't it?' She rose from her seat and fished out her phone. 'I'll call Phil now.'

'No,' he reached forward to grab for her wrist.

Kate snatched her hand away. 'Don't do that.'

'I'm sorry. I didn't mean to get rough. I'm just really worried.'

'I know,' she answered. 'That's not okay though.' She handed a ten-pound note to the coffee shop manager and forced a smile. 'Thank you.'

He followed her to the door and out into the street. Neither seemed too concerned that they were standing amidst a windstorm.

'Tell me about Johnny McCabe.'

Garry's face darkened. 'Her attacker. Three years ago, he broke into our house. My parents were at their timeshare in Menorca and I was on my first tour in Afghanistan. He'd apparently been following her for months. She said it seemed innocent at first. She'd run into him at the supermarket and he'd offer to help her home with the shopping.' Garry looked past her, as if seeing it playing out in front of his eyes. 'She didn't need the help; she was fit and able. She was just too damn polite.'

Kate squirmed. She knew all too well the feeling of being violated, of having your sense of worth destroyed in one fell swoop.

'That's when it started to get more intense. He delivered a gift to the office she worked for her birthday. Everybody she worked with teased her like mad. They thought it was hilarious that this creep nearly twice her age had decided to make her the object of his affection. That's when her anxiety became obvious. She'd come home upset that he'd follow her into bars when she was meeting friends. Everybody tried to convince her it was innocent.' A look of guilt as his lips drooped. 'Even me.'

Kate reached forward and rubbed his bloodied hand. 'I'm sure Charlie doesn't blame you.'

'I blame myself.' He rubbed at his face, evidently in pain. 'I should have warned him off, beat the crap out of him and told him to stop deluding himself. Maybe the humiliation would have forced him to leave her alone.'

'Or maybe it would have only made his intent more violent. Never believe you can reason or threaten someone like that into stepping back.'

He cringed. 'Mum didn't want to go away. She kept saying Charlie didn't seem herself. She was hiding away in her bedroom, sneaking about, spying out the curtains. It wasn't normal. Dad said she was an adult and she had to face her issues. There was no point them babying her.'

Kate shuddered. She tried to imagine how Charlie's parents must feel now.

'He broke in on the Saturday night, caught her off-guard as she came out of the shower. He forced her to the ground, raped her and then stabbed her in the chest. He appeared to be this nice guy who violated my sister and then left her for dead. If he hadn't been seen running away from the house, leaving the door open, she might not have been found on time.'

'Oh my god,' murmured Kate, hiding her lips behind her hand. 'Poor Charlie.'

'It took us a week to convince her to go to the

police. Then another fortnight of sheer hell when everybody learned what had happened. It was nothing compared to the trial though.'

Kate wasn't sure she wanted to know any more of the details.

‘Four bloody years he got, out sooner if he was good. I'm only surprised they didn't hand him a fortnight in the Canary Islands. They practically blamed her, accused her of leading him on. His lawyer asked her why she had accepted expensive gifts from him and implied it entitled him to expect something in return. Listening to that, I had to run to the bathroom and vomit.'

'You don't think Johnny McCabe's got anything to do with Charlie disappearing?'

‘I’ve never heard that he’s been released. He’s incorrigible though. He wrote to her months after going to prison, asking her to visit him, telling her that he knew she’d been forced into reporting it and that he forgave her.'

‘Forgive her?’ It was Kate’s turn to feel sick. 'Is that why she moved to Glasgow?'

'Yeah, moved to Glasgow and took my mother's maiden name. Living in hope that if he does manage to get out of prison that he won't come looking for her.'

'Surely there are conditions he has to follow if he's allowed parole?'

'You would think so. I don’t think she's convinced though. That's why she remains on hyper-alert.'

Kate hailed down a taxi that suddenly appeared from the mist. ‘I don’t think we have any more time to waste. Charlie might be in trouble and we can’t afford not to get the police involved.’ She stepped into the vehicle and mumbled their destination. Then she and Garry fell into an awkward silence that wouldn't be broken until they arrived at the station.

39.

The killer walks to the last lock up in the block, blue paint peeling from rusty steel doors before he swings the key into a rotting padlock. The car was deliberate, but the early discovery has hastened him along. He now must act a little swifter. No more time to play.

He didn't want infamy at first. That desire came later. His goal was to avenge what he'd lost, and to pay back those who had failed him. Those people will be singing a different tune when they see him on the news. Everybody should know his name. They'll want to know why he's killed four women. Has there been a thought process? A motive? Has he chosen them randomly or is there a reason for it? What will he say? The stars have guided him, probably. Though it cuts deeper than that.

There is this issue to deal with first. It will only be a matter of time before the old drunk hands his name over. Leads them to the lock-up. To the car. To his DNA. He's driven that car a hundred times, long before he ever knew it would be his destiny to kill those girls. There isn't a fibre of fabric, or inch of the steering wheel that doesn't have a part of him moulded into it. He must stop them from getting to it. At least until he finishes what he has started.

The killer grabs an empty red can and pours a bottle of petrol into it until it is half full. As he does this, he lowers his nose because it is a scent he has long enjoyed. When he is content that he'll have enough for the task at hand, he throws open the boot and slips it into a tight groove. Beside it, a pair of fearful eyes blink at him, the wrestling of arms in ropes too tight to break, a moan from behind a cleave gag made of old cloth. One leer, the pressure of his hand over the captive's drooling mouth and there is silence. The killer, satisfied he's made his point, slams the boot shut again.

It is almost two miles to the house. It is a journey he could make blind folded. He thinks of his third victim, the one who almost thwarted his plan by having her stupid thick-headed brother show up. She'll likely still be wriggling in the dirt, working out why she's been targeted a second time, most likely attributing her plight to the man who had destroyed her life in the first place. Will she realise just how off base she has been?

Back to the job at hand though because he doesn't have much time. He eyes himself in the rear-view mirror, content with his current self. Then he mentally ticks her off in his head. He senses she won't be dead yet. She is feisty, probably has a few hours or a day left in her body, but she'll never survive the oncoming storm that has been promised.

Three down, one to go.

The final girl is a doozy, the one who confirmed to him he wasn't making a mistake; a masterclass bitch. He doesn't even know if he has the patience to let her freeze to death. He might just break her swan-like neck. The other ones should be chicken feed by comparison.

He tightens his hand round the steering wheel, slamming down on his accelerator and feels his inner rage flush the surface. He is doing ninety in a car that should rightfully be scrapped, which won't be necessary. It has one more purpose to serve first.

The killer turns left and drives along the dirt road, the car rattling like a tin can in a tornado. The wind batters past him but barely makes a dent in his speed. A little storm isn't going to get the better of him.

He pulls up outside the farmhouse and smiles. The last time he was here, his little critter of a stepfather was completely unaware of his presence, not knowing the man he turned into a killer was looming over him. This time, Kenneth Black won't be so lucky.

40.

'Hello, my name's Detective Phil Morris. I'm with Glasgow division. The reason I'm phoning is in connection with the disappearance of a young woman originally from Aberdeen. I believe she was previously involved in an assault case that you might be familiar with.'

'Sure. Can I take your badge number?' Her voice was hoarse and flattened by her thick Aberdonian accent. She had simply introduced herself as Barbara.

Phil fumbled before reading out the number. 'Sorry about that,' he continued. 'You'd think after thirty years on the job I would remember my own identity number.'

'No problem,' she laughed. 'What's the person's name?'

'We know her as Charlene Westmore, but I think that might be her mother's maiden name. Her brother's name is Garry Shanks.'

'Charlene Shanks?'

'I think so,' said Phil, having already despatched a team to head straight to Charlie's house. He might have been slower to react if not for the fact her disappearance wasn't unlike that of Michelle and Beth's. Except this time, they were being given a head start.

'I remember her all too well, darling.' The woman paused so that only the sound of the keys tapping could be heard down the phone. 'She's from a small village just five miles from here. Nothing much happened there before she was attacked. It was all anybody talked about when the trial was going on. You wouldn't have treated a dog the way his legal team treated that girl.'

Phil had already got the gist of the details from Kate. He didn't feel it was necessary to ask the woman to elaborate. 'I just want to know about her attacker. What prison he's in? When he's due for release? Are there any other known victims?'

'Listen, darling. I'm going to have to call you back in a few,' she said, her voice becoming more dramatic as she spoke. 'Can you leave your number with me?'

Phil hated to be kept waiting. It was one of his many flaws. 'Of course,' he said, through gritted teeth. 'Do you know how long? We really are quite concerned about this young lady's safety.'

'Tell you what I'll do, Detective Morris. I'll pop you on a silent hold and go and speak to one of my seniors. It may take a few minutes, but it'll save us playing phone tennis later.'

Had she said her name was Barbara, he found himself wondering? It sounded like she'd said Barbara anyway. If not, he'd just call her that anyway. He didn't want the indignity of now asking her name, five minutes into the call. *Thanks Babs*, he thought to himself, picturing her a chain smoking, coffee-swilling hag who took in stray cats on her days off.

During those silent moments, Phil rattled his pen on the desk, whistled that damn song he'd heard on the radio for the past week and tried not to make eye contact with Donna who was now giving him a look of irritation. Finally, he heard a click on the other end of the phone.

'Detective?'

Aw, Babs, you're an angel.

'Yes, I'm here.'

'Okay, some bad news for your young lady. Her

attacker, one Jonathan McCabe was released on licence about seven weeks ago. The good news is he's still having to check in with us.'

'Wait, I thought that the victim was supposed to be notified of his release, and essentially any local agencies that she's involved with.'

'It says here that a message was left with her parents. That was on the eighth December.'

'Her brother says the parents are away. I'm not sure if they would have gotten the message. You've had no way of contacting Miss Shanks herself?'

'When you say concerned, how?'

'I'm not sure yet, though I am in the middle of investigating the murder of two young women who are similar ages. One of them works in the same place as Miss Shanks. I don't like coincidences, if you get my drift.'

'I don't believe in them myself.'

'She's disappeared. Her brother showed up in town a few days ago and is staying with her. He says he was out all night and when he got back to her flat, there seemed to be a disturbance. When he contacted her work, they'd also not heard from her and her boss seems quite worried about her.'

The woman he'd come to know as Babs, sighed. 'Garry Shanks?'

'You know him?'

'He created quite a fuss over her attack. Naturally so. He's her brother but many was the time we thought we might have to arrest him for disturbing the peace. Thank goodness they locked McCabe up when they did, or I think Mr Shanks would have done him in with his bare hands.'

Done the world a favour, thought Phil. 'Maybe so. According to my fiancé, he's quite the hothead.'

'Nice fella,' she acknowledged. 'I can imagine he's hard to control though. I'm glad he's your problem today and not ours.'

'If he was my only problem,' continued Phil. 'I'd be a very happy man. Right now, I'm more worried about Charlene. When was the last time McCabe checked in at the station?'

Babs cleared her throat, whispered something inaudible and banged on the keyboard once again. 'Yesterday. Last time was the eighteenth January, before that the eleventh.'

'Which makes it tricky for him to be in Glasgow at the times we're talking about.'

'Are you thinking that Charlene's disappearance is related to your dead girls?'

Phil smiled. There were no flies on Babs. 'I don't have a conclusion yet. The two women disappeared on the twelfth and nineteenth, but there had to be activity in between.'

Babs must have read his mind because she then offered him the next favour before he'd even fully thought of asking. 'You want us to send the hit squad round to have a word, find out his whereabouts on those days and determine whether he's had any contact with Charlene?'

'That would be superb. Thank you,' he said, enthusiastically.

'I mean, there's nothing to say he isn't responsible for her disappearance whilst having nothing to do with your dead women,' continued Babs, the cold voice of reason.

'Absolutely. I'm not ruling anything out. Whilst I've got a mad man on the loose in my city, I have to plunder every scenario.' Without further conversation, he said goodbye and reluctantly ended the call. Truth be told, he was already wishing that Charlie's disappearance was at the hands of McCabe and not whoever was carrying out the cold killings of those young women. At least then Charlie would have a chance.

~

It always amazed Phil that such an air of gloom could fall upon somewhere as light as Charlie's bedroom. A train of chocolate eyes glared from within a hammock stuffed full of soft toys. The room itself posed little concern save for the fact it looked like the bedroom of a child. 'All three girls slept in bedrooms that make them look as if they're stuck in a time warp.'

'Perhaps that's why he chose them. Emotionally stilted people are much easier to prey on,' reflected Donna

They edged past a team of forensics assigned to pick apart every fibre of evidence and put together a picture of Charlie's last movements. A crime scene photographer aimed a 35mm camera in every direction so they could later recreate the room in minute detail.

The bathroom probably held the most evidence, its stillness the aftermath of something intrusive and violent. Whilst one analyst hovered over the sink, dusting for fingerprints, the other muttered into a Dictaphone, talking himself through the crime scene as if reliving Charlie's every traumatising minute.

Phil was certain they would only find what the killer wanted them to find. He had already taken two women in the cold light of day without anyone coming forward to say they'd witnessed it. Then he'd managed to drop them into a pit without leaving anything by way of evidence. That was a tricky feat, particularly when the weather was so against him.

‘Did you know her brother arrived back from his last tour just a few days before Michelle Evans disappeared?’

‘You don’t think he’s involved?’

Phil shrugged. ‘If you had told me before Charlie went missing that he arrived back in town right before the deaths started, I might have looked into him.’

‘Not now?’

‘You saw how distraught he is. Besides, I get the impression he’s fiercely protective of his sister.’

‘I think he’d kill Johnny McCabe in cold blood if he got his hands on him.’

‘Do you blame him? If I had a sister and someone did that to her, I don’t think you’d be able to piece their body back together. There’s a difference between a psychopath and a distressed relative exacting revenge.’

‘You’re defending murder?’

‘Never. I’m saying I can relate to that a damn sight more than what’s happening here. I’m certain McCabe has nothing to do with any of this though. I don’t think there’s anything to gain by hauling over what happened to Charlie in Aberdeen. If we really want to know what’s happened to her, I think the key lies in whatever went on once she arrived in Glasgow.’

41.

When she woke from an all-too-brief slumber, Charlie was sure she could hear something above. Before she'd nodded off, she had been listening for the sound of the car engine. The rain had evidently stopped because it no longer battered against the wooden slats. However, the wind was more ferocious than ever, leaving her in fear that her makeshift hole might be ripped apart any second now.

She twisted in the space causing a tiny shift in the surrounding cocoon. The pain in her skin had eased off, presumably because she was no longer being lashed by shards of rain. However, her face still felt as if someone had poured flames on to it.

As she tried to get more comfortable, fearful to leave her new haven, Charlie suddenly heard a scratch. Where she hadn't been sure before, it became evident she wasn't alone.

Had he returned while she slept? Why had she allowed herself to sleep? She was just so damn tired, and her gut had long since begun to tingle with hunger. She quickly quashed those concerns though because she sensed someone was standing over her makeshift grave.

Charlie held her breath, fearful that when she next exhaled it might not escape. She turned her head to glare into the darkness. At the end of the space she could see the hole, just big enough for a man to climb out of. Or in.

He blinked.

Charlie let out a scream, a tsunami of terror rising to pour over her. 'Help me!' The words hung heavy in her chest but didn't manage to formulate.

He was coming in, oblivious that the grains of

dirt were now falling through the gaps in the wooden slats and pouring into every crevice of her face.

Charlie felt as if she was beginning to suffocate, her throat burning as the dirt unloaded freely onto her naked body. She let out a muffled scream feeling as if gravel was rushing to her lungs.

He cackled. The voice was familiar. She would never forget it. Johnny McCabe, a man who had stolen her life and she'd never had the opportunity to take it back. She thrashed wildly then, finally finding the fight that had evaded her until now.

'I'll never let you go this time,' he crowed, the voice of a mad man.

She managed to wrestle her hand up and grabbed for his face as it slithered closer. Another scream. Then she opened her eyes and found herself lying beneath the calm damp slats.

Charlie was sure she'd been awake. He seemed so close to her. Even now she could smell his breath and taste the falling grains of dirt. It wasn't real, she realised. She must have been dreaming, or hallucinating.

The winds were as wild as they'd been a moment ago, the rain still poured down and Charlie still felt like her skin was burning up. How was that possible when she felt so cold? She needed a breather from inside her cocoon, so she shimmied forward towards the hole. As her mind calmed, she realised something else. She would recognise the smell of Johnny McCabe anywhere. It was etched in her brain. She could even hear his disgusting breath, the one that had landed on her as he took every ounce of her dignity. She didn't recognise any of that on the night she was taken. She didn't know who had captured her and put her in this dismal place but the one thing she was becoming certain of, Johnny McCabe wasn't her attacker this time. She looked up to the rolling clouds, her eyes still barely focusing and silently begged god to take her right now if she was destined to die.

42.

It was less than an hour before Phil heard the raspy drone of Babs' voice. The woman had wasted no time on dispatching two uniformed officers to go and have a word with Johnny McCabe. McCabe, a shivering weasel of a man, cowered behind the door, looking terrified that they were coming to take him back to prison.

'I genuinely don't believe he's got anything to do with her disappearance,' insisted Babs.

'Did you speak to him?'

'No,' she replied.

'With all due respect, Barbara, you're basing an awful lot on someone else's intuition. Did your officers get into the house? Did he allow them to look round? Remember this is a man who broke into the house of an innocent young woman, violently raped her and left her scarred for life.'

'I appreciate that, Detective Morris. However, you probably never heard Charlene Shanks' name until this week. My officers took her through the process, made the arrest, comforted her poor mother when she looked as if somebody had sucked the soul out of her body and stopped her brother from committing murder. I trust my colleagues to be able to assess a situation without the need for me to turn up and cattle prod them.'

'My apologies,' said Phil, feeling suitably chastised. 'I wasn't inferring they didn't know how to do their job. I just need to know that he's not got Charlene holed up in his basement or a hut somewhere.'

'He looked absolutely terrified that his bail was being revoked when the officers arrived at his house.

I think, even if he wanted to commit another attack on somebody, prison has been enough to deter him.'

'And he was able to account for his time on the days I asked you about?'

'Absolutely,' answered Babs. 'He's learning IT skills at a local centre that helps ex-offenders and homeless people find accommodation, or work, or claim benefits if that's what they require. He goes there every weekday between the hours of ten and four. I just checked in and he's signed in for all the days of the week, including the days you asked about. He also said he hasn't been near the Shanks house, which leads me to suspect he doesn't even know Charlene's left town.'

'If I'm being honest, that's the news I dreaded to hear. I hoped your officers were able to find her there or at least get some indication that he knew about her disappearance. You're sure they were thorough?'

'I believe they would have been. I asked them not to mention anything about her disappearance, but they were fully briefed on what you told me and on her ordeal. They didn't go in there with the intention of mollycoddling him.'

Phil cradled the phone in the grip of his palm for a moment longer before deciding to accept what Babs had told him. At least it was one box ticked off in his investigation. 'Thanks, Barbara. I have a few other avenues to explore. I'll be back in touch if I need anything else.'

Another call was already sneaking in when Phil ended the call. Carrie's number flashed as the handset vibrated in his palm.

'Carrie?'

'I'm sorry, I'm still working on that hair for you.'

Phil groaned and then laughed grimly. 'That's

the kind of day I'm having. Do you know how much longer you'll have to wait?'

'I'll make it priority as long as nothing else comes in.'

Phil ended the call, feeling slightly irked that nothing was going his way. He wanted something concrete that they could get Kenneth Black in on. At least the chief had promised them their warrant to search the farmhouse and its surrounding land. If Charlie were to die as quickly as the other girls, Phil already suspected it was too late. They had not another moment to waste.

43.

The figure wriggles in the tiny space, ankles wrestling frantically against the knots, moaning loudly from behind the gag to be set free.

However, the killer isn't focused on the winsome groans for attention. He is watching something else, a man standing in the doorway with a bottle in his hand. The killer is seething. There is no remorse in the old man's stance, nor in the twisted leer of his expression.

The land is flat, the corns in the dead fields flying in a seventy-mile per hour gust. It looks just as bleak as it did twenty years ago, except the man in the doorway is old now.

The killer winces. He stares at the sky, searching for her, aching for her approval. After all, he has done all of this for her.

Another moan from inside the car.

The killer slams the boot door down and the old contraption shudders loudly. He walks towards the old man, momentarily reliving something dark and ungodly. He feels the shadows at his back, brushing up against his spine, spurring him on to finish what he has started.

'What have you done?' The old man's mouth is moving, the voice frailer than the killer remembers, his gait rendering him vulnerable.

The killer stomps up onto the porch and knocks the bottle from the man's hand. He doesn't utter a word because he learned long ago that silence would fill a man with more fear than any words he could ever utter.

The old man is about to turn away, the same look of disgust that once instilled terror in the killer.

The killer peers past the old man, see's nothing much has changed in the hallway of the farmhouse and jams his foot between the closing door and the draft excluder.

The old man looks surprised. 'You finally found your balls? Who's in the boot of my car?'

The killer merely smirks. He sees the surprise on the old man's face, hears the slight apprehension in his voice. He hears the manic voice in his head congratulating him on finally facing the one thing that he'd never been able to.

He surges forward, quickly bringing up his hand to the man's neck.

The man stutters. 'What are you doing? Don't put your hands on me, you scrawny little bastard.'

The killer isn't scrawny anymore but for a moment he is transported back in time. Here lies my childhood, he realises, dragging the old man back out of the house that haunts him still.

'Let me go,' says the old drunkard, his arms thrashing wildly.

The killer still doesn't speak. His face is contorted by a lifetime of growing malevolence. His demons faced, the past eradicated, the killer pushes his tormentor towards the green Volkswagen. For a moment, he wants to gloat; to celebrate this moment that feels like he has finally taken back what is his.

The old man is ranting now, drunken slurs that remind the killer of the days gone by. A family reunion accompanied by murder.

The boot door is now open again; a length of rope fished from beneath the writhing body inside. The killer is wrapping it round the old man's wrists now, pulling so tight that no amount of whiskey will numb the pain.

'What are you going to do with us?' The old man's rants have been momentarily halted, and he stares at the terrified eyes of the younger captive.

The killer grabs the red petrol can and slams the door once more.

The old man stretches his neck but must realise the danger he has found himself in. So, he ceases to fight back and allows himself to be placed in the front seat of the car. There's a look of horror matching the realisation that he'll be lucky to escape alive.

The killer pulls the seatbelt, loops it once round the tied rope and locks the old man's wrists firmly in place. Not originally a part of the plan, but the killer is quite pleased that today Kenneth Black, will face his maker. The killer grabs the red can from atop the car and begins to douse the old man in petrol.

The old man pulls frantically at the seatbelt, one last frantic bid for freedom. The knots are too tight.

The killer reaches into the old man's pocket and pulls his cigarette lighter out. Finally, he speaks because this moment deserves a brief sermon. 'This will be painful, but it'll be over in less than five minutes. Which should be long enough for you to appreciate the years of pain you gave to me and my mother. I did consider locking you down in the well as you did to me, but four days doesn't seem long enough to repay what you have done.'

The old man's eyes widen more in desperation. He wrestles against the seatbelt. Finally, he appears to accept his fate, knowing his stepson will grant him no mercy. Instead, he spits at him, a ferocious act of final defiance.

The killer sparks the lighter, drops it on to the old man's lap and turns away. As he climbs a wire fence to take a short cut back to his own vehicle half a mile away, he stops and looks back. Just for a second he enjoys the unearthly screams of his burning abuser.

44.

Kate didn't know when she first realised she was being followed but half way up Byers Road, having left Garry at the same hotel she and Phil had spent the night in, she suddenly became aware of someone behind her. Her pulse quickened as she mentally revisited a time where she had known what it was like to be followed. The feeling never changed.

It took a lot to bring Byers Road to a standstill, but Storm Maggie had managed it. Only a handful of patrons lingered in bars whereas many shops were now taking the advice of the media and closing their doors. Even when she passed the door of a coffee shop she had visited for the past three mornings Kate didn't bother to stop and exchange a pleasantry. She was too aware of the footsteps now edging closer to her.

She turned her eye to the corner, her neck perfectly rigid and her footsteps quickening. Up ahead, she could see the corner that led along Highburgh Road. It wouldn't take her long to get there, but the only question was, if she was being followed, would she make it there before being accosted.

A second later, the owner of the footsteps came into her side-view. A man in a long black coat, a bonnet and a lopsided gait rushed past her. He nodded to her, quickly appeasing her and silently promising that she had nothing to fear.

Kate wanted to apologise. How stupid she felt. As her face reddened, she allowed the man wide passage and then stopped to catch her breath. Maybe the storm was starting to get to her. Maybe the knowledge that a killer was lurking somewhere on the streets of Glasgow made her feel less safe than she had in a long time. Or maybe she just needed to get a grip and stop seeing potential abusers where there were none.

As she turned back to continue her short journey, Kate suddenly heard her name being called. She spun round just in time to see a figure reach forward.

'Hello, fancy seeing you here.'

She jumped quickly to anger. 'Alan? What the hell do you think you're doing? Are you following me?'

He looked wounded, stepped back and threw up his hands. 'No! No! Not at all. I only just caught a glimpse of you and wanted to apologise about yesterday.'

His words didn't soften her. She was raving mad that he'd intruded in the refuge yesterday and made her look ridiculous. 'Where were you? I didn't see you.'

He pointed to a quiet little café a few doors back. 'I'm in there with my partner.'

'Partner?'

A man emerged from the doorway.

'Yes, you know him. Doctor Luke Murdoch. I believe you take one of his classes?'

Kate caught her breath and realised that if she already felt stupid, it was nothing to what she was feeling now. 'You're gay?'

Alan let out a howl of laughter. 'Very much so.'

Luke stepped in then. 'The only thing surprising to me is that you're surprised. He's an old screaming queen. Hello Kate, how are you?'

She was still smarting from the fright he gave her but managed to muster a smile. 'I'm fine. I just, erm, I just didn't expect to see you here. I'm rushing back to the refuge.'

'At this late hour?' Alan fiddled with his scarf and pulled at the lapels of his jacket.

'It's only after eight and I still have a few things to do there. I had to leave earlier to take care of something.' She didn't want to mention where she had been to Alan as she had already learned just how indiscreet he could be. Besides, she didn't think it was wise to discuss Phil's workload with someone she barely knew or respected. She may well say too much to a man who she didn't trust one iota.

'Come and have a coffee. I feel that I've upset you in some way. I'd like to treat you to a coffee or a tea and apologise for being a little overzealous.'

Kate squinted. She wasn't sure that she was ready for a sit-down with Alan yet. She was still smarting from the way he took her confidence and railroaded over it.

'Please, it's on me. Then we can walk you along the road to the refuge. You look like you could use an escort,' said Alan.

Luke snorted. 'She doesn't need an escort, you buffoon. She's an adult, not a dog.'

Kate laughed then. It was nice to see someone giving Alan a little taste of his own medicine. 'Okay, but it'll need to be quick. And it better be a good coffee for me to forgive what you did yesterday.'

Alan, looking sheepish, took a little bow and followed them back into the café.

45.

The second drive to the farmhouse was more tumultuous than the first had been. The elements now stood firmly against them, rain battering on the window, so the windscreen wipers were swinging full pelt. The wind howled so wildly that the car wavered back and forth and almost veered over the lines a few times. Phil checked the rear-view mirror to ensure that his tag team were still on route. He watched Donna rustle the warrant in her hand and looked forward to wiping the drunken scowl off Mr Black's face.

Phil was still on the dirt road when he noted the bright light and billow of smoke rising into the sky. 'I don't believe it,' he muttered.

'What?' Donna followed his gaze and allowed her jaw to drop.

As he drew closer, he saw that the flames rose and blew only a few yards from the front of the farmhouse. 'Thank god,' he said. 'At least it's not the house that's on fire.'

Donna gasped as they pulled into the long driveway. 'No, but I think it might be the car we've been looking for.'

The front of the green Volkswagen had become a fiery ball, greeting them on their arrival, taunting them with evidence that might never be.

'The sly bastard.' Phil parked on the other side of the farmhouse, far enough that his own car wasn't at risk from being engulfed in flames. His rage became boundless. 'If he thinks this gets him, or any accomplice off the hook then he's got no idea just how determined I am.'

Donna rushed round the car, shaking her head

and handing him the warrant. 'Doesn't he realise this only implicates him further?'

'Sometimes they think they're being clever. They haven't the brains they were born with.' Phil pulled his mobile phone and hit speed-dial for the fire service.

One of the other officer's grabbed for a small extinguisher and lunged towards the fire.

'Be careful,' shouted Phil, reluctant that his officers should battle the fire at all. 'If that engine explodes, I wouldn't want to be in your shoes.'

'Mr Black?' Donna was rattling on the door now. 'Kenneth?'

When there was no reply and the house appeared to be in darkness, Phil stepped forward and thumped harder. 'Mr Black, we've got a warrant. Whether you open the door, or we break it down, we're coming in.'

No reply.

'Do you think he's in?'

Phil smirked. 'Passed out drunk, probably.'

Donna carefully turned the knob on the door and listened to it creak open. 'Not very careful of Mr Black considering how ungracious he is about visitors.'

Phil suddenly felt apprehensive. He recalled how unwilling Mr Black was about letting them in earlier. He'd hidden behind the chain at first. Now, his door was unlocked for anyone to walk in. Donna was right, he wasn't a gracious host. The threat of a warrant had frightened him enough to burn out the old car, but not to lock up. That didn't make sense. Why leave the door open? 'Step back a second, Donna.' He beckoned at the young Sergeant on duty. 'I'm not sure how safe this is. Can you fella's lead the way?' Stepping out of the way to let four uniformed officers holding batons into the house, he waited for the all-clear.

Donna beetled in before him, leaving him last to enter the farmhouse. The stench from earlier seemed much worse now, though there were also no lights to welcome them.

As the other officers searched the rest of the house, Phil heard one of them shout down the stairs. 'No sign of anybody here. The house is empty.'

Phil stared outside, the light of the dying fire now dimming. He could also hear sirens in the distance. Even by small town standards, the fire service was quicker than he expected. 'I'm going to check out that barn,' said Phil, eager to know what horrors might hide in there. 'Now we've got a warrant, there's nothing stopping us from searching the entire land. We don't need him to be here and we don't need his permission.'

'What do you hope to find?'

'Charlie Westmore,' he answered, no tone or hint of humour in his voice.

'Do you really think we'll find her? Here?'

'It makes more sense than Johnny McCabe travelling back and forth to exact revenge when they're saying he's frightened of his own shadow.'

Donna shrugged. 'He didn't use his own land for the other bodies. What makes you think he'd have brought Charlie here?'

'The car's here, isn't it?'

Donna was following him through the gale, wrapping her jacket round her chest. 'I'm still not buying Kenneth Black for this. He's an old bastard, but capable of murder? It doesn't ring true. Somebody unconscious is a dead weight. I don't even think he could carry a body with someone else's help.'

'I know, but I still feel like he's protecting someone. A son, maybe? Why else set that car on fire right after we brought it to his attention? Where is he now? He knows we're coming back so why disappear if he's got nothing to hide?'

Finally, the rotten steel chain fell from the barn door handle, allowing them to enter. There was little in the barn of note. An old battered truck with four flat tyres slumped at the centre of the stone-cold shell, probably not used in a decade and in dire need of someone to push it back to life. Dusty shelves adorned the back wall, playing home to a hoard of paints and solvents. At the barn door, a pitchfork, a hoe and a rake. Not exactly the industrial tools required for a land of this size. Not that it looked like anyone had done any upkeep in a long time.

Donna stepped round the truck, shining the torch from her phone so that she had a visual. 'Do you think this farm ever produced? No animals, all the crops dead and not even a working truck. Why have a land like this and not make money from it?'

'He probably inherited it. It looks like he preferred a life on the booze rather than actually working for something.' Phil stepped back out of the barn as he heard something clattering from behind the barn. Little more than a stone's throw away he could see a small turret poke up from the ground. 'Donna, bring your phone until I have a look at this.'

She came out of the barn, keen to see what he was looking at. 'What is it?'

'I don't know, looks like a well or something.'

As the two of them approached it, peering into the abyss he took her phone from her and shone the light round a red brick circle. He reached for a half full bucket and pulled it to the edge. 'Rainwater,' he concluded, letting it fall so it battered against the brick side. As he nested the light against the soggy walls, bleak from years of damp he grimaced into the deep hole.

'Can you see anything?'

Phil hushed her. 'Nothing,' he replied. Suddenly, he heard the voice of an officer as a silhouette rushed towards him.

'Chief, you've got to see this.'

'What?' Phil stepped away from the edge of the well and moved to meet the officer.

The officer looked grey; his face haunted by whatever it was he was coming to share. He leaned on his knees to catch his breath. As he looked up, he shook his head in horror. 'A body, in that car. Somebody was in the front seat.'

Donna gasped!

'I'm guessing they're dead. Nobody's going to survive that.'

'That's not all,' said the officer.

'What else?' He didn't need an answer though because he turned just in time to witness a body being lifted from the boot of the burning car.

46.

Garry's face felt like stone, his lips like ice as he stormed through the doors of the police station.

His sister's flat had been turned into a crime scene and he had been forced into a hotel whilst the police tried to put together a timeframe of her disappearance. Garry had left three voicemails on his friend Tony's voicemail begging for a bed but found that his pleas had fallen on deaf ears.

'I want to speak to Detective Morris.' He wondered if the man behind the counter could smell the alcohol on his breath after he necked half a bottle of whiskey neat.

'Name?' The uniformed officer behind the glass sheet didn't look very impressed by Garry's arrival.

'Garry Shanks. My sister is missing, he's investigating her disappearance.'

The officer appeared to groan under his breath, but not inaudibly enough that Garry didn't hear it.

'Sorry, I know you're only doing your job. I'll not get in your way of that,' he snarled, slamming his fists on the counter.

'Steady, fella,' replied the officer, a middle-aged man with a receding line of grey hair and facial features that looked like they'd been drawn on by a cartoonist. 'Detective Morris isn't here right now. He's working a case now. I'll see if someone else can help you. What's your sister's name?'

'Charlene Shanks, or Westmore,' said Garry.

'Well, which is it?'

Garry felt stupid quite suddenly. He hadn't known about Charlie's assumed name until recently and it still felt strange to be using it. He hadn't really questioned it. Now he wasn't sure what name they would be searching under. 'Westmore,' he finally said, eagerly.

Without another word, the officer slammed the window shut and picked up a cordless phone.

Garry perched himself on the counter, cocking his head to try and hear the conversation whilst also enjoying that he was dirtying the window with every breath.

The window finally slid back open. 'I don't know when Detective Morris will be back. He's very busy but if you want to wait here, someone will come out and speak to you.'

'When will that be?'

The officer stuck his lower lip out and shrugged. 'When they get to you? Now wait here and behave yourself.'

Garry wanted to thrust his fist down the man's throat, inform him that he defended Queen and country but the last thing he needed was to be arrested now. For once, he cooled his hot head and stood away from the window. He wondered about Kate, the woman who'd seemed so concerned about Charlie and wished he had taken her own personal number. He wasn't sure she'd still be at the refuge as time was ticking by. He turned to the clock. When had Charlie been taken, he wondered? It had been twenty-four hours since she'd stormed out of the pub. It could have happened any time after that. Garry felt a pang of guilt. Why had he not understood how upset she was? If he'd accompanied her home, she'd be safe now.

Selfish prick, he thought to himself.

He wrung his hair out with his hands and headed back to the door. 'I'm out here for a smoke. Don't forget about me.'

The officer nodded and continued to fidget with a pile of unfiled paperwork.

Garry walked towards the door, despaired and desperate. As he lit his cigarette and inhaled it deeply, he looked at the sky. 'Charlie, where are you?' He wouldn't hold back the tears any longer. He felt them tickle his cheeks, warming his skin as he shivered on the steps of the police station. Then he made a vow to himself. If a hair on his sister's head was harmed, nobody would hold him back this time. He would commit murder with his bare hands.

47.

'I seem to have upset you in some way,' acknowledged Alan, once the waitress had delivered three hot drinks.

Kate didn't speak. She simply eyed his expression, wondering if there was anything genuine behind that blinking façade.

The café itself was as pretentious as it looked from the outside, hanging baskets above every table, hipsters reading the riot act on an increasingly disturbed world and an abundance of clashing aromas from a giant hissing coffee machine.

Kate groaned to herself and returned her gaze to the man with the handlebar moustache.

'It was presumptuous of me, haphazard even. I shouldn't have come to the refuge without speaking to yourself or Natasha first.'

'No, you shouldn't have,' interrupted Luke.

'You could have made me look really bad,' said Kate, finally prompted into a confrontation.

'I'm sorry. Please don't let this get in the way of me helping you with your final dissertation. It's important to me that you do well.'

Kate frowned. 'Why?'

'He likes you, silly,' said Luke. 'Believe me, he doesn't like many students.'

She looked at him suspiciously. 'Why not?'

'I don't cope well with pretence. When they come into the lecture theatre, they look at me like I'm some sort of God who is going to magically instil intelligence in them. They think if they are learned enough, it'll mask their ignorance of everything else, all the things they deem frivolous and uninspired.'

'What if that's all I want?'

'It's not. Every time you've been in one of my lectures you've looked at me like I'm a God damn irritation, an inconvenience, as if you're waiting for me to get to the crux of my point. In fact, you're doing it right now.'

Kate gasped! A little laugh escaped, and she watched a smile formed on Luke's face.

There, revealed, was the true face of Alan Groundwater, a man whose demeanour and vocabulary were at complete odds with who he now claimed he wanted to be.

'I'm not looking at you like anything,' she insisted, laughing a little more.

'I'm not annoyed, Kate. I find it refreshing. You're honest and you're not pretending to be something you're not. If I didn't have to engage the minds of hundreds of those very people I am venting about, I would like people to find me honest and refreshing. It's a lovely notion, but not so attainable when you have a certain expectation placed on your head.'

She leaned forward and blew into her mug. 'You're not expecting me to feel sorry for you, are you? You're one of the cleverest people I've ever met. When you're in that lecture theatre, you're commanding the attention of every person in the room, whether it's adoration or irritation. You don't have students, Mister Groundwater. You have fans.'

He snorted. 'Fans?' His snort turned to a full-on guffaw. 'I like that. My adoring fans. What is the opposite of that? My critics?'

'Probably,' she answered, matter-of-factly.

'Now look what you've done,' said Luke, mockingly. 'I've already got to live with this man's ego. Can you imagine how much more unbearable he would be if he takes that to his head?'

They all laughed then; the ice broken on a frosty relationship that seemed doomed from the outset.

'So, Alan tells me your partner is a policeman. That's exciting.'

Kate nodded. 'A detective. He'd tell you it's not as exciting as it sounds. Long days, trawling through horrendous conditions like those today to solve some of the worst crimes you can imagine.'

'It sounds fascinating,' said Luke, staring at her. 'What is he working on now?'

She glanced past them, stared into the rain and wondered how much longer a killer would be allowed to walk the streets. 'You know those two women that were found murdered? The ones on the news over the past couple of days?'

'I saw something about that on the morning news. How tragic, and in this horrendous weather. They didn't have a chance.'

A shadow passed over Alan's face. 'It is tragic. I knew Michelle Evans. She was a lovely girl, a very good student in fact.'

Kate gulped. 'You taught Michelle Evans?' She leaned forward, clutching her phone and feeling the urge to instantly call Phil.

'Yes,' said Alan. 'She had only just moved to Glasgow. In fact, I believe she might have been the first or second person who did a placement at Marina Cullen House.'

Kate felt her heart race slightly. 'We didn't find any record of her ever working there.'

'You probably wouldn't. Back then, we controlled the student placements rather than the organisations we placed them with. Now, it's all GDPR and disclosure, so it means of course that the organisation must have a paper trail of anybody working or volunteering there.'

'Natasha went through her files with a rake trying to find any history of Michelle working there.'

'Why is it important?' Luke looked intrigued as he knocked back the last of his coffee.

Alan appeared to have already made the connection. 'Did the second girl also work there? I don't think I know her.'

Kate suddenly tightened her lip. 'I don't think I can say too much at this point, but I really think I need to call Phil. This is the connection he's been looking for. He'll probably want to talk to you.'

Alan nodded. 'Of course. I didn't know that I knew anything the police didn't.' He looked genuinely quite pleased with himself, as if he was suddenly going to be included in something that the rest of the world wasn't privy to.

'You can't say anything to anyone now. A lot of the details are being kept away from the media.' Kate pulled her purse out and fished a five-pound note. She placed it down on the table and turned. For a moment, she felt a little guilty though. So much so that she turned back to look at Alan. 'I'm sorry I was off with you. I'm sure you're a nice man but sometimes I've felt very uncomfortable around you.'

He smiled. 'I hope we can change that.'

She was about to leave when she thought of something else that Phil had asked about. 'Mister Groundwater,' she said.

'Alan, please,' he insisted.

'A lot of your students talk to you about things other than their studies, don't they?'

A nod of the head.

'Did Michelle Evans ever tell you about someone

she was having a relationship with?'

Alan looked like he was mulling over all the confidences that had been shared with him. As if breaking his code of privacy was a real test of his conscience. 'Oh shoot, I suppose it doesn't matter now. Anything that can help. Michelle met someone when she was there. Someone who was involved with the refuge in much the same way as I am. You know I like to dip my toes in it, though Natasha hasn't been receptive to my involvement.' He looked disgruntled by the snub. 'Anyway, Michelle seemed quite excited at first. I did ask who it was, but she said he wanted to keep it a secret for a while.'

'Was he married?'

'I don't know,' replied Alan. 'It didn't take long before she was talking about going home. I wondered if it had just fizzled out.'

'Did she never say who he was?'

Alan shrugged. 'No, I'm afraid she didn't. I don't even know if it was a male. It could have been one of the females. She never mentioned it again for as long as she was attending my classes and I never asked. I didn't feel it was any of my business. You don't think it's related, do you? Not after all this time.'

'I don't know,' answered Kate. 'Did she never mention anything about this person?'

Alan paused, pensively staring into his mug. 'Oh, god, yes she did. She said the person was working undercover on something important. It was all rather cloak and dagger but, as I said, it all seemed to fizzle out so quickly that it was never mentioned again.'

Kate thanked them, hit the dial button on her phone and prepared to make the dash from the café to the refuge. All the while, as puddles formed round her feet, she couldn't help but wonder if Michelle's secret had come back to haunt her with a vengeance.

48.

Phil slammed the door, so it was only himself, Donna and Steve in the incident room. He had not received the outcome he wanted. Right now, he hoped to be returning Charlene Westmore to her brother. Instead, he had a burned body in the mortuary and another unidentified body in a coma.

'So, we know the tied-up body in the boot wasn't Kenneth Black because he's probably about thirty years too young. So, who the hell is he?'

'Another accomplice?' Steve turned to Donna and lifted his shoulders.

'I doubt it. Accomplices don't end up locked in burning cars. I think somebody discovered what the killer was up to.'

'How did uniform discover there was somebody in the boot anyway?' Phil could still smell the smoke on his clothes and couldn't wait to get home and get out of those clothes. The thought of warm steaming water bounding down his skin was appealing. Having Kate climb in to join him was the cherry on top.

'Martin heard the banging and the muffled screams. It was him who managed to get the boot open before the car was blown sky high.'

'Just in the nick of time, from what I hear,' said Steve.

'It was close,' acknowledged Phil, still reeling from the explosive sound of the car spiralling into the air. 'It's going to be a delicate process identifying the driver.'

'You're sure the burned body belongs to Mr Black?'

'At this point it is pure conjecture. It could be anybody. Maybe Kenneth Black is far from his farmhouse, accompanying whoever it is that he's been protecting and moving onto their next victim. Until we know who burned up in that car, I don't think we should rule anything out.'

'Maybe it was him and he killed himself to avoid capture.' Steve slapped a pen against the palm of his hand.

'You think he might have set himself on fire?' Phil's eyes narrowed, incredulous to the point of laughter. If he wasn't so damn fed up.

Donna squirmed, pulling a handful of photos from a brown folder. 'There wasn't much of value in the house, certainly nothing to suggest that Kenneth Black was our killer. Though, the master bedroom was a little more interesting. A cupboard full of badly damaged toys including a smashed telescope, some ripped up astrology books and a broken bunk bed.'

'The telescope looks old.'

'One of the books was an astrology guide to ninety-ninety-nine. Maybe it belonged to one of Kenneth's kids.'

'There's been no mention of children, but I'm still convinced there must have been.'

'There must be a connection between the astrology materials and the star branding left on the victims. I keep going back to the fact that Kenneth refused to give up whoever had access to his car. He knew exactly who it was who was using it, I could see it in his face.'

Donna bridged her front teeth on her folded fingers, looked intensely at the board and nodded. 'Maybe he didn't know. If he's protecting a son, he would do that instinctively without necessarily knowing that it had been going on. We really need to pin someone down on the name of any children he fathered.'

'If it is a son he is protecting, it's a strange way to repay loyalty, lighting someone on fire. I can only think that an act like that comes from a place of hatred. I could never understand someone killing their own parent but any I've ever seen have at least had a modicum of care. Setting someone on fire is pure rage filled.'

Donna gulped! 'Care? Not usually a word I associate with someone killing their dad. Remind me not to say no to my kids next time they ask for fizzy soft drinks.'

'You met Kenneth, Donna. Without passing too much judgement, he's one of the foulest human beings I've had the misfortune to meet. Can you imagine having a father like that?'

'There's a report that states his wife committed suicide. Did I read that right?'

'Yes, but no mention of a child.' Steve continued to slap the pen against his hand. He stopped when he noted Phil's irritation. 'Sorry.'

'Nothing mentioned in any of the police reports. This cupboard,' Steve pointed to a photo, '-is filled with paraphernalia that looks like it was owned by a boy. It's all in the cupboard of the master bedroom. The three other bedrooms upstairs were practically empty, old shackles with single beds and nothing more. It certainly doesn't look like a house filled with love.' He faded into the background, a line forming on the ridge of his nose. 'Why would there be no mention of a kid if the police attended several domestic complaints there?'

'This was twenty years ago. Laws on domestic incidents left a lot to be desired. Maybe social services might have gotten involved though,' offered

Donna.

'I'll call South Lanarkshire and see if I can speak to a duty social worker,' said Phil.

'We can't stop searching for Charlie though,' insisted Donna. 'She's still out there, still in danger and if the killer knows we're on his trail, it might just force his hand. I dread to think of her still out in this torrential weather. If she isn't already out of time, she soon will.'

'Finding Charlie is number one priority. I want every resource we have on it. There's no question of giving up. Her brother is waiting in one of the interview rooms. I want to know everything he knows about his sister's life. I also want to know if he can shed any light on a connection between Michelle, Beth and Charlie.'

'Did Natasha over at the refuge confirm if Michelle ever worked there?

As if on cue, Phil's phone rang. Kate's image flashed up. He quickly pulled the phone to his ear, heard her breathless tones and the lashing of rain all round her. 'Slow down, Kate. So, you're telling me that Groundwater remembers Michelle being his student.' He allowed Kate to finish telling him her discovery before whispering that he loved her and ending the call.

'What?'

Steve and Donna moved closer to him as if they were going to be included in a massive secret.

'Michelle was placed by the university at the refuge. At that time, it was only a requirement of them to hold records. The refuge wouldn't have been required to keep those records prior to GDPR. Natasha wouldn't have been the manager back then. However, the Professor has said that Michelle was definitely seeing someone and that she was keeping her cards close to her chest.'

'Did he say who it was?'

'From what Kate said, he doesn't know. All she said was that this person was working on some sort of case. Which makes me think that the killer we're looking for is probably one of our own.'

Donna's eyes widened. 'You think it's a copper?'

Phil's heart sank. The only thing that could make this case worse was arresting someone he might have respected or worked with in the past. 'Did either of you ever feel like this killer was always one step ahead of us? The minute we got on the trail of Kenneth Black; he was murdered. When we learned about the car, it was burned up. The killer knew our every move at the same time as we did. I don't know if it is one of our own that's doing this, but I think whoever the killer is, they're getting an awful lot of bloody help.'

49.

Garry clicked his fingers repeatedly until he heard the door click open. 'So, you're Phil?' The man was older than he expected, especially considering how much younger Kate was. Not what he was expecting at all. In other circumstances, in a bar perhaps he might have commented on how Phil was punching above his weight. He buried the thought, caressed the twitch at the corner of his mouth and crossed his ankles.

'Nice to meet you, even if the circumstances aren't ideal,' said Phil, sitting directly across from Garry.

There couldn't be a worse situation for an exchange of pleasantries, thought Garry, refusing to partake.

'What happened to your face?'

Garry eyed Donna, unsure whether she was sympathetic to the bruises on his face or assuming he was a thug deserving of the beating he'd taken. 'Ran into a bus.'

'Tricky,' said Phil, almost good-humouredly. 'Can you talk us through the last time you saw Charlene.'

Garry blew lightly, chewing back the urge to roar that he'd already gone through this earlier. Losing his temper wouldn't help. The sooner he told them what they needed to know, the sooner they could get out and find his sister. 'She was working all day at the refuge, but came to meet me and my friend at the pub.'

'Your friend?'

'Tony Morgan,' answered Garry, realising how everything irritated him right now. 'Charlie was on edge, as she often is in social settings. I tried to get her to relax, you know, told her to have a drink and let her hair down.' He poked his own aching ribs, feeling a tingle in his gut.

'Did she?' Donna leaned back in her chair, sniffing and running her hand across the rim of her nose.

'No, she wasn't interested. Now that I think about it, it was obvious she didn't want to be there, but I'm such a shit head sometimes. I nagged her to come.'

A silence developed in the room, no comfort offered, no effort to appease Garry's growing guilt.

'So, Charlie left the bar before you?' Donna broke the silence eventually.

'We had words. I try to encourage Charlie to move on with her life. I know what happened to her was terrible, but I don't want her to let it drag her down.'

'The attack?'

'Exactly.'

Donna held her hands up, the shadow of her fingers growing across the table. 'Who says she has to move on from it? You? Society? Who gets to decide how long before she must get over what happened? Nobody else has the right to make that call.'

Phil's brow wrinkled. 'What bar were you at?'

'Ringo's on Byers Road,' he replied.

'What time did Charlie leave?'

'Not long after she arrived. I would say at approximately eight.'

Donna shook her head. 'That's not long after we saw her at the refuge.'

'You saw her?'

'We were there on a police matter,' offered Phil.

'Charlie must have been on her way to meet you.'

'I feel terrible,' said Garry, feeling his voice break. 'If I had just offered to walk her home.'

Phil tusked. 'No point blaming yourself. If someone intends to harm Charlie, they'll find a way.'

Garry's ears pricked up. 'I'll kill anyone who harms her. You can document that wherever you need to.' He swung back on the chair, causing the two front legs to momentarily lift from the floor.

'You're in the army, aren't you?'

'Yes,' replied Garry, failing to see what his own occupation had to do with anything.

'What does Tony do?'

'He's the same as me, though he was discharged a few years ago.' He paused. 'PTSD.'

'What does he do now?'

Garry shrugged. 'Consultancy work, I think. He doesn't really talk about it. I don't ask.'

'Is it legal?'

'I don't ask,' repeated Garry, emphatically.

'So, you and he stayed out drinking until what time?'

'No, I stayed out alone. Got talking with a few girls, ended up in a brawl, hence the smashed-up face.'

'No bus then?' Donna smirked.

She looked a little sour-faced, but she was growing on Garry who liked a woman with a smart mouth. 'You know how it is, never one when you need it.'

'When did Tony leave?'

Garry took a second to think about it. 'Around the same time as Charlie. He's a bit of a lightweight these days.' His mind returned to his friend who had been AWOL since his sharp departure that night.

'Have you spoken to him since?'

Garry tapped on the table, a seed of doubt suddenly growing from his inner mind. 'Not directly.'

'Or not at all?' Donna was reading his expression now.

'He has nothing to do with Charlie's disappearance if that's what you're asking?'

'Anybody who has been in contact with Charlie could be a suspect, or a credible witness,' said Donna, pointing at a folder that lay before them.

Phil slipped some of the photographs from Charlie's upended bathroom onto the table. 'Has Tony ever been to Charlie's house?'

Garry squirmed, recalling Charlie's anger when she learned that he'd brought Tony over. 'Once.'

'So, he knows where she lives?'

Silence.

'Garry, your sister is missing and we're really quite worried for her safety now. We need every bit of help you can give us. You're telling us that Tony knows where she lives?'

'Yes!'

'Is Charlie seeing anyone?'

Garry laughed then, a hearty spurt of laughter that lifted the tension immediately. 'Absolutely not.' He angled himself directly across from Donna. 'She was sexually assaulted in the worst way possible. I'd be surprised if my sister ever looks at another man in her lifetime.'

'Did she and Tony get along?'

'They didn't really know each other.' Garry flinched. 'Why all the questions about Tony. I've known him for years. He's a good mate. I'm not concerned for my sister's safety around him. I'm more concerned about where she is now.'

'I understand but we have to look at every person as a suspect. Particularly those who were the last to see Charlie before her disappearance. How much do you know about Tony's background?'

Garry had to think again. Tony tended not to talk much about his childhood. He seemed to have a rocky relationship with his father and he'd once mentioned his mother had died when he was young. Save for that, not many of the army boys had managed to get much out of Tony. Instead, he spent his time cracking jokes, which Garry had long since suspected was a mask for whatever deep-rooted pain he felt. 'I don't really know how to answer that. He's just a mate. He likes a laugh and a good drink. He doesn't really have any family. I felt a bit sorry for him. He came and spent Christmas with my family a few years ago.'

'Did he and Charlie get on then?'

'I think they get on fine.'

'Can you give us Tony's number? We just want to speak to him briefly. Rule him out, if you like.'

Garry reached into his pocket and pulled out his phone. As he looked at his dialled list, he saw he'd made more than twenty calls to Tony since the morning after Charlie's disappearance. There had been no response. He suddenly felt apprehensive. Had he been trusting of someone he shouldn't have been? Tony had always had his back in the past, a loyal friend to the bitter end. Yet, Garry realised he didn't really know Tony very well. 'I think you're barking up the wrong tree,' he said, reading the expression of concern on Donna's face.

Phil rose from his seat. 'It's purely routine. We'll want to speak to him and anyone else who last saw Charlie.'

Donna followed him to the door. 'When are you

due back at base?'

Garry couldn't even think of that now. If Charlie didn't turn up in the next few days, he'd be asking for a leave of absence. 'Supposed to be soon. I doubt that'll be happening. I've got other things to take care of.'

Phil patted him on the back. 'Make sure you leave it to us. I appreciate how desperate you must be but there's no point getting yourself arrested.'

Garry had already warned of his intentions. He didn't think it required repeating. He simply nodded and made his way back onto the cold, wet streets.

50.

Kate had finally calmed down when she walked up the path of Marina Cullen House. As she approached the entrance, Rochelle and little Danny Walton were coming towards her. Kate smiled.

'Don't even speak to me,' hissed Rochelle as she threw open the door and shook her finger.

Kate felt a surge of shock ring through her. 'Pardon?'

'You pretended to be our friend. Worse than that, you pretended you were like us and that you understood what it was like to be me.'

'I do,' stuttered Kate, trembling.

'Then why did you arrange for a psychiatrist to come and diagnose my son with a psychosis. Do you have any idea how difficult it was for me to come here?'

'I know how difficult it must have been.'

'No, you don't, you patronising bitch. You have no idea what it's like for us to have to wake up here. Our lives have been ripped apart and we've got nothing. You've got your big brave fiancé, your five-star wedding coming up and a life that we couldn't begin to imagine.'

'I know what it's like to have nothing. I promise you; I didn't arrange for anyone to come and diagnose Danny with anything. I spoke to my lecturer about his symptoms…'

'Symptoms? What the fuck are you talking about? Are you honestly this stupid? My son is not ill. He's traumatised.' Her voice must have been travelling up the steps because someone was now rushing down them.

'What's going on here?' Natasha appeared inside

the hallway, holding out her hand to appease Rochelle and usher them all back inside.

'I'm sorry,' mouthed Kate.

'Rochelle, sweetheart. Come back inside and we can talk. It's not a night to take Danny out in,' Natasha said, her voice the gentle contrast to her earlier firmness with Garry Shanks.

'You know, Natasha. You should really be careful who you let slither in here. You're supposed to be keeping us safe, not letting predators like her use us for her own advancement.'

Natasha moved between them. 'Sweetheart, that's not what happened. Kate didn't even know the professor would turn up here, but I promise you he will not be setting foot in the refuge again.'

Kate felt her face flush, despite the chilly wind belting against it. 'I honestly didn't, Rochelle. I would never do that.'

'So, who suggested he had a mental illness then? Did that professor see it in a dream? One of you must have told him about Danny for him to come here in the first place.'

Danny pulled into Rochelle's leg, hugged it tightly and groaned. 'I'm hungry, mummy.'

Despite both Kate and Natasha's attempts to dissuade her that any harm had been meant, Rochelle picked up Danny in her arms and rushed towards a car waiting at the end of the path. The door swung open and Danny began to scream violently.

Kate saw a man emerge from the driver's seat and slam his hand on the bonnet of the car. She recognised him. There was no mistaking his six-foot frame, mass of dark hair and thick beard. He'd been outside the day before. Maybe little Danny hadn't been imagining things after all. One more notch on her guilt post.

Rochelle looked back, defeat firmly spread across her face. She had come to Marina Cullen House in trust and that trust had been betrayed.

Kate's guilt would later eat at her but for now, there were more pressing issues at play. She wanted to speak to Natasha about Michelle Evans. Perhaps there was something else that she might learn now that she knew the girl had been a student there.

'She's going back to her husband,' said Natasha, the first time a melancholy edge had passed her voice.

Kate knew it too. They'd heard the screams of that little boy and she'd known it right away. His father, the brutaliser in their home had come to collect them so even if Kate and Rochelle had ironed out what had happened, the refuge would no longer be safe for Rochelle or Danny. Kate had unwittingly pushed Rochelle into a corner.

Natasha moved towards Kate. 'We can't have another thing like this happen, Kate. I know you didn't mean for this to happen, but I just hope that nothing happens to Rochelle or Danny. I fear that you're going to have enough trouble sleeping.'

51.

When she raced out of her cocoon, Charlie wasn't sure whether he'd seen her or not. Her vision was still nothing more than moving silhouettes. The engine had also been quieter than the one she'd previously heard which made her wonder if it really was her captor returning to taunt her.

Charlie had been dreaming, or hallucinating. She wasn't quite sure because each minute merged into the next without her really knowing what was real and what was not. Earlier she had been sure she heard the voice of her brother, calling to her, lifting her to safety. She had wept when she realised it wasn't real. Real, salty, painful tears.

'Charlie,' he called, a taunting drone that was just audible enough for her to hear.

She looked up, squinted her eyes because she remembered being a child and tightening her eyes into one of those magic eye kaleidoscopes. It worked then, but barely made things any clearer for her now.

On her hands and knees, Charlie knew he would expect her to be in a state of near death. She had to give him a little of what he wanted otherwise he'd suspect she'd tricked him.

She could see him leaning over now. How she wished he'd fall, break his neck or his back. Anything to debilitate him and give her a chance of survival. Even now, fear subsiding and giving way to defeat, there was still a little trickle of hope because it didn't appear that he'd discovered her hideout.

'Charlie,' he hissed, this time loud enough that it echoed round the edge of the rotunda. He was tormenting her, his voice carried sinisterly by the wind.

Charlie recognised the voice, just as she thought she recognised his eye when the memory of her attack had returned. Yet, she couldn't put her finger on it. Not yet. She slid forward in the mud, determined he wouldn't know she was gaining strength rather than wilting. She heard him cackle then, a vicious unyielding laugh at her expense. She knew he hadn't touched her. She knew the sensation of a sexual assault all too well and that hadn't happened this time. Why had he put a distance between himself and her? She couldn't understand it. Then she heard him say her name again.

'Charlie Farley,' he sang.

She gasped. There was no mistaking it. She recognised not only the playful way he sang it to her, but the unique moniker itself. Only one person had ever called her it. Her face tingled, from the burning sensation round the edge of her eyes to the frozen tug on her aching chin. The rest of her simply froze. She knew exactly who had taken her hostage.

~

The killer doesn't know whether to be angry that Charlie is still alive or impressed by her tenacity. She has outlived his first two victims and doesn't appear close to dying yet. How can this be? It has been minus five for the better half of a day, yet she still scrambles round in the dirt, an ant clamouring for food and shelter.

It won't be long now, he reassures himself, amused by the comparison to an ant. He knows the investigation into the first two murders may soon start to yield results but they're not as clever as he is, not as astute or tuned to the elements as he has always been. Yet, he still finds himself wondering why she isn't dead yet?

The killer feels cheated. The murders haven't quite captured the attention of the media in the way he'd hoped. He had also set himself a rigid timeframe, today being the day that victim number four would be taken. Within days, all four would be dead and discovered but Charlie had ensured a detour in his plan. Still, he was cranking up an impressive body count and he suspected it wouldn't end at the original four. The beauty of unspent plans.

He was singing her name now. If nothing else, he wants the pleasure of her knowing who he is. There's no mistaking the expression on her face as he delivers a melody of old. 'Charlie Farley,' he sings. He's prodding her now, like needling the back of a dying wasp. He knows she knows, and it fills him with elation. Someone finally knows who he is. Who better to reveal himself to than the one he loves the most?

He recalls the moment she'd spun round, right before becoming unconscious. He had been certain she would recognise him. That was okay though, because she wouldn't be alive long enough to share his identity. Now he knew she hadn't recognised him at all. That moment where they met face to face had been all too brief and it had taken his special pet name for her before she finally knew who had taken her.

Even from this height, the killer can see her disgust. It doesn't faze him. He holds the power in his pale dark hands. Her story may have moved him but only for a moment because, despite what she has endured she has never known what it was like to be truly tortured. Not like he knows. As they hurtle towards the final act, knowing that he may have to intervene and kill her with his own bare hands, he twists the neck of a large grey bottle. She'll have the same snatch of hope that the other two had but only for a moment. He snorts to himself and twists the tight black cap.

~

Charlie heard him speak as she saw the shape of him holding something out.

'I suppose you're thirsty,' he growled, no longer bothering to conceal his voice.

Though she couldn't really see it, she could hear the thrash of the liquid pouring onto the ground. She felt desperate. She had almost forgotten what clean drinking water tasted like. It was just one tiny lifeline as she battled to survive. She lunged forward, her knees hitting the ground again and cupped her hands. No sooner had she filled her hands than she brought it to her lips. Thankfully, Charlie caught the scent just in time. She looked up.

He continued to pour.

Charlie's face filled with horror. 'You're a monster,' she howled, trying not to let him see her resolve break. She heard him chuckle, a sadistic grind from behind clenched teeth. She threw the liquid to the ground, scrambling back so it was completely out of reach. Then she dipped her hands in a nearby puddle to wash the petrol off.

'Don't worry, Charlie Farley,' he said. 'I'm not going to burn this hole up just yet, but I will be back.'

52.
25th January 2019

At just after two p.m. the next day, the storm finally hit its peak. Ninety-mile winds carried thick sheets of rain, drowning trees and powerlines across various parts of the country. As the famous Clyde rose to overthrow boats and crash onto the side paths, many homes were dropped into darkness. The streets were evacuated, whereas businesses were thrust to a halt. The city of Glasgow came to a complete standstill.

For Phil Morris, it was business as usual. He had a killer to catch and not even the deadliest storm in fifty years was going to stop him now. It had taken the best part of the morning for him to locate a social worker who had been with the South Lanarkshire team when Kenneth Black was reported for abusing his wife. Now, all he was waiting on was a call back to confirm there had been a child and, therefore social work intervention. All he needed was a name.

'Steve, I need you to go back to Kenneth Black's house and do some more digging. The local constabulary have done their bit and its back to us. Donna, can you go as well?'

Donna nodded first, Steve following as he awaited her approval.

'Is there anything we're looking for?' Donna scribbled quickly on her notepad.

'Anything that will lead us to Charlie,' he replied.

'Won't the house still be sealed off?'

Donna laughed. 'No, the crime didn't happen inside the house. Forensics have done their bit and the car has now been taken away so they can try and pull as much evidence as possible. The only thing they've managed to salvage from the car is the remnants of tarpaulin from the back seat and the man rescued from the car boot.'

Phil rose and swept past them. 'I wonder if he's awake yet. It would be helpful to know who he is and to find out if he saw where they might have taken Charlie. I might head over to Hairmyres. I just hope Charlie's still got some fight left in her.'

'I hope so,' agreed Steve. 'We will need to find her soon. Tonight's the night for Maggie to do her thing.' He looked out the window and sighed.

Phil ushered them out as his phone began to vibrate. 'Great, it's Carrie. I hope she's got a name on that hair they found on Beth.'

Steve and Donna both disappeared, neither seemingly eager to accompany the other but probably realising that Phil was at his wit's end with them both.

'Carrie?'

'Hey, sorry it took so long for me to get back to you. There was a massive horror smash over on the Clyde expressway at the weekend. Three teenager's dead.'

'I heard something about that,' he said. 'What a waste.'

'I know, it's the families you feel it for. Anyway, back to the matter in hand, I do have a name for you.'

Phil's heart leapt. 'Thank god. Go on then, let's have it.'

'His name is Anthony Morgan, thirty-five-year-old male from East Kilbride.'

'Tony Morgan,' re-iterated Phil. 'He's a friend of Charlie's brother. Do you have any other information on him?'

'Afraid not. The next part is up to you.' She

paused.

'You've gone quiet. Everything okay?'

She blew into the phone. 'I went over Beth Phinn's body with a fine toothcomb. I don't know how I missed the hair the first time.'

'No harm done,' mused Phil. 'Listen, Carrie. I appreciate you getting back to me. I'll let you go for now. It looks like I've got an arrest to make.'

53.

An eerie silence hung over the car as Steve and Donna drove straight into the centre of the mist. Dust kicked up against the side windows, whilst the streets looked as if Armageddon had already be-fell them. People were locked away, not because they feared death at the hands of a killer now dubbed Rain-man by the media, but because they feared injury by falling roof slates or overturned garden furniture.

Steve hadn't spoken in more than ten minutes and Donna didn't feel too aggrieved by it. In fact, she was relieved the aggravating small talk had finally trailed off. She twisted her right eye in his direction, noting how he tightened his grip around the leather steering wheel.

They drove into a row of naked trees, the windy screech battering against the windows. The sky above was barely visible now, replaced by an endless stretch of clawed branches that hovered over them as if welcoming them into the bowels of hell.

'I'm still at a loss as to why he doesn't just kill them himself. He's got them there in his grasp,' wondered Donna, breaking the silence with a question that had loomed heavily for over a week.

'Maybe that's no fun.'

'It's just laziness if you ask me. He wants the notoriety but doesn't want to work for it,' she snarled.'

'It almost sounds like you want him to kill.'

'That's a stupid thing to say,' she snapped. 'Are you sure this is the right way? I don't recall coming this way the last time?'

Steve didn't say anything, he simply tapped on the screen at the centre of his dashboard so that the map lit up. Then he rubbed his hands round the steering wheel and glared into the distance.

Donna eyed him suspiciously. Not for the first time she wondered what his background was. Since he'd joined the team, he had talked a lot but said very little about himself. The stillness behind his eyes had unnerved her on occasions and she found herself wondering again what went on back there.

'What?'

Donna turned away, flushing suddenly. 'I didn't say anything.'

'You were staring.'

'Was I?'

The car throttled over a bump in the road, breaking the awkward exchange and causing her to let out a shallow scream. She laughed then; the ice broken once more.

'I like Charlie,' he said, throwing it out there as if they'd been talking about it all along. 'She's feisty. A survivor, you know.'

Donna suddenly got the sense there had been more intimacy between the two than she first realised. 'You knew her well?'

'Well enough,' he replied.

'I didn't realise. I know you were involved with the refuge because Phil said you got Kate the placement there. That was decent of you.'

'I introduced Kate to the refuge, but it was actually her lecturer who suggested it.'

'Did you introduce Charlie as well?'

'No, I helped Charlie when she first came to Glasgow, but she was already working there when I met her. She was like a mouse, barely speaking and shuddering at the very sight of a man. I thought she was a resident at first. I gave her advice. It was me who suggested she change her name because she was terrified her attacker was coming to find her.'

'You don't have to look very far to find the worst of humanity.' Donna squinted as the car hurtled into darker terrain.

'I was sorry to hear about your mother.'

Donna felt her shoulders tighten. 'How do you know about that?' Had Phil betrayed her confidence? Once upon a time she would have doubted it, but Phil had almost taken Steve under his wing recently. Or was it the other way around? It was hard to know anymore, but this latest betrayal of her confidence felt like a gut punch.

'Sorry, was I not supposed to know? I overhead Phil talking about it.'

She didn't want to know any more. Nor did she want to have the conversation with someone she disliked so intensely. She had to change the subject. 'Let's just find Charlie. I want to deliver good news to her brother and her parents. They've already lost her once; I don't think they should have to lose her again.' There was a haunting edge to her words that swept through her until she shuddered. When she looked at Steve again, she saw his jaw line had tightened.

'We're here.'

Donna whipped her neck round as the car hurtled to a sharp stop. She felt herself thrown forward but then pulled back by the mighty grip of her seat belt. Any more force and she might have found herself bruised across her chest. 'Jesus Christ. Are you trying to kill us both?'

He leaned forward and wiped away condensation on the window. 'Did you see that?'

Donna looked outside, her gut twinging as she

eyed the dark, bleak farmhouse which was now a deserted crime scene. 'What?'

'The window upstairs. Someone was standing there.'

Donna felt a chill spread through the car as she clutched her chest. 'I can't see anybody.'

'They're gone,' he continued. 'There was someone there a second ago.' He reached for the car door and pushed it open against the wind.

'What are you doing?'

'The man who owns that house is most likely dead. The only other person we've been able to associate with the place is probably the killer we're looking for. This could be our break.'

The cynic in Donna couldn't help but to feel slightly aggrieved that Steve was about to land the gold. Yet, it would mean an end to the Rain-man murders. Surely that was the priority above all else. 'I'm coming with you,' she said, despite her growing fear. She turned to look at the house again, shadows from the sky spreading across so it looked even more like a shack than it previously had.

'No,' he lifted his hand in defiance. 'Don't come with me. You stay here in case anything happens to me. There's no point us both going in when we don't know what we're going in to.'

Still, Donna couldn't find it in herself to trust him. Despite her intense dislike of him, she was also reluctant to allow him to put himself in danger.

Steve must have detected her reluctance because he raised his eyebrows and smiled. 'Don't tell me you're actually concerned about me.'

She sniffed. 'Hardly. If you want to get your head hammered in, knock yourself out. We have protocols to follow though and it's my neck in the noose if they find out I let you go in there alone.'

He giggled awkwardly, clearly biting back his nerves. 'Put it this way, if I come out alive there'll be nothing to report. If I end up dead, who will tell them any different?'

'Not much comfort,' she admitted.

Steve shook his head. 'You're a hard woman to get through to, Donna. Look, give me two minutes and if I've not given you the nod that I'm okay, you call for back up, okay?'

Finally, she agreed and watched him race through the barricade of rain before he disappeared into the old farmhouse.

54.

As he thumped hard on the door, Garry could hear someone fumble with the lock inside. 'Tony, it's me,' he shouted, dripping wet and more intoxicated than he'd ever felt in his life. He fell against the door as it was pulled open.

'For Christ sake, Garry,' said the man who stood in his underwear. 'You've woke me up. What the hell are you doing here?'

Garry pushed through the door. 'Where's Tony?'

'He's not here,' answered the other, a figure of skin and bones who still held on to the latch of the door. 'He hasn't been home in a few days. I thought he was with you.'

'He buggered off and left me sitting in the pub.' He shook his head in realisation. 'Wait, what do you mean he's not been home in days? Where the hell is he then?'

'I'm his flatmate,' answered the gatekeeper. 'Not his husband.'

Garry barged up to Tony's bedroom door and thumped on it.

'I told you, he's not here. Stop fucking banging. I've got a headache.'

'My sister is missing,' said Garry, feeling his anger begin to wild out of control again. 'Somebody took her.'

'Shit! When?'

'Same night I last seen Tony.'

The gatekeeper finally slammed the door, grabbed a filthy grey t-shirt from a nearby hanger and covered himself up. 'Have you reported it?'

'Yes,' barked Garry. 'The police were very interested in why Tony disappeared right after Charlie left the bar.'

'He won't be involved. That's ridiculous.'

'Is it? Then, where is he?'

'I don't know,' stuttered the other man. 'You know he goes off on binges. Probably partying somewhere.'

Garry sighed. 'It's an awful coincidence. When he gets back, tell him I need to speak to him.'

'Sure, Gaz. I'll tell him to phone you.'

Garry rushed to the front door and pulled it open, trying hard not to breathe life into the dread that was growing in him. Yet, he couldn't bury the knowledge that if Tony had done something to Charlie that it was he who had put them in the same room. If Charlie didn't survive this, he'd have himself to blame but there would be nothing anybody would be able to do to stop him from killing Tony. He took the stairs two at a time, preparing to brave the tornado of winds that swayed the lampposts, crashed against the stillness and had basically turned the city into a ghost of its former self.

55.

Phil felt the black grip of grief the minute he walked into the house. What struck him more than the gloom was that the house had stayed perfectly still since the first time he'd been there. A dirty teacup sat perfectly still on a porcelain saucer at the side of Marilyn Phinn's armchair, the photo album she'd pulled off the shelf when she learned of her daughter's death still askew on the middle of the table while the same grey outfit still clung to her skinny hunched frame. Phil half expected to look at the clock and see that it had stopped at 3.27pm which had been the time they'd delivered the news to her. Hers was now a world frozen by grief.

'How are you holding up?'

Marilyn didn't look up, nor attempt to wipe her eyes, now a glacial blue behind the tears.

Phil noted the one thing that had changed was just how gaunt she was. What little colour there once had been was now replaced by an ashen blue. If she hadn't opened the door to him, hadn't muttered a throaty 'hello' and hadn't moved before his eyes, he might have sworn she was dead as well.

'Like someone's run over me with a tractor,' she finally mumbled, her words wrapped in the kind of pain that could only be reserved for a childless mother.

'I'm sorry,' he whispered, leaning towards her. 'It's a stupid question. I'm sure you're sick of being asked.'

'Nobody asks,' she informed him, lifting her head quickly. 'Do you see this room? There's nobody here. There was only her and I,' she continued bitterly. 'There's not queues of casseroles, people lining up with flowers or an unmanageable pile of devastating cards. Liz from next door popped in on the first day with a pot of soup and told me to knock on her door if I needed anything.'

'That was kind,' acknowledged Phil.

'It was. Except we've never stood the sight of each other in twenty years. Isn't it ironic though that the only person who does turn up is the one person who you wouldn't give daylight to?'

There was no point mithering round the subject, so Phil decided to speed himself along. 'You know the other day when we asked about Beth seeing someone, it's come to light that there was a person in her life. I know you said you weren't aware of it, but could Beth have mentioned anyone in passing?'

'No, it's as I've told you all before. We barely talked. Beth lived her life and I allowed her to. Don't get me wrong,' she continued. 'There was a time when we were extremely close. She was like my shadow. For the past five years, it was like living with a stranger. I always expected that if I gave her enough freedom, she would come back to me one day.'

Phil nodded, noting the lack of expression in Marilyn's face.

'I had an overbearing mother, you see. I didn't want to be one of those horrendous needy mothers who don't let their children breathe...' Her voice cracked, as if suddenly realising the enormity of what had taken place.

Phil lurched forward, placing his hand on hers but she snatched it away so quickly he didn't have time to feel for any heat from her skin. 'Have you ever heard the name Tony?'

Marilyn's eyes rose. 'No. Should I have?'

'I don't know,' he said. 'We're pursuing a few

lines of enquiry now. He's just one person of interest.'

'I'll have to make this really easy for you, Detective because I'm exhausted and to be honest, I don't know how many other ways to say it. Beth didn't introduce me to friends, I never heard her talk about boys, and I do not know where she went other than when she said she was going to college or work.'

Phil could tell when he was being clipped but he wasn't about to be browbeaten so easily. 'What about her father? There hasn't been any mention of him.'

Still her expression didn't change.

'Dead,' she snapped, quickly closing any potential for further discussion.

'Dead? Or just gone?'

For the first time, Marilyn's eyes narrowed into a tame form of anger. It quickly disintegrated. 'Does it matter? Beth never knew him. He's dead to her.'

'I'd still like to speak to him,' insisted Phil, gently.

'There's no point. Anyway, I wouldn't know where to find him. No doubt he'll see it on the news and come swimming back like the piranha he is. Until then, I'd rather not speak about him or hear about him. It'll be traumatic enough when he finally shows his face.'

Phil stood, no longer able to suffer the hang of the bleak atmosphere. He wondered if this was what it felt like to step into a black hole and have the soul sucked from the body. Or buried alive. The oppressiveness was beginning to seem suffocating. He took a deep breath, eyed the little slither of light that pervaded the side of the curtain and thanked her for her time. 'I'll be going now. Detective Barclay will check in with you tomorrow. I believe you have her mobile number so if you need anything, just call.'

Marilyn sniffed. 'I can't imagine what I'd need.'

'Donna's your family liaison officer. She'll want to support you in any way she can. Don't hesitate to use her. That's what she's there for. And if you remember anything at all that you haven't told us, it doesn't matter how trivial it is Marilyn, call us right away.'

She attempted a smile, but her lips didn't seem to know what to do. Her eyes were permanently glazed over now and there was little chance they'd operate for any other purpose than to drain her of every grainy emotion.

When Phil saw her move forward, he held up his hand. 'Don't see me out. I'll be fine. You take care.'

Still, she rose from the seat, her hands quivering as she pushed herself to her feet. 'When will they release my daughter's body? I want to start making arrangements.'

It was one of the most frustrating questions Phil could be asked. They didn't even have a suspect yet. There was little chance of those girls being put to rest until the investigation was complete. 'It's hard to say. Obviously, we'll push for it to happen sooner rather than later. We don't want to prolong your agony any more than we need to, but it is important that every shred of evidence is documented and that we're able to revisit anything we've missed. You understand?'

She looked like she didn't, but she merely nodded in exhaustion.

Phil exited the way he entered and took a deep lungful of air. He couldn't remember in all his years of policing a place so devoid of life. He leaned against the stone balcony and felt the cold whip round his neck. Then he heard a voice.

'How's she holding up?'

Phil spun round, startled because he hadn't realised there was anybody there.

A woman, likely Liz from next door emerged from under a dim orange light. 'Sorry, did I give you a fright?'

'I don't scare easily,' he said. 'You must be Liz?'

'I'm the battle-axe next door. No doubt she told you how much we dislike each other. Not strictly true. She dislikes me because my kids are rowdy, and I didn't chain them to a chair.'

'Oh,' said Phil, recalling Marilyn's statement about their difficult relationship. 'So, you really don't get on very well then. What about your kids? Did they get on with Beth?'

'Not really,' answered Liz. 'She was a bright girl. Very studious. She was a little out of place in this block. Not that I minded her. She was always pleasant, never walked past without saying hello and offered to help me up those stairs with my shopping when the lifts were out a few times.'

'Shame you never got on really. What age are your kids?'

'Eldest is twenty-five, my twins are seventeen and the youngest, my menopause baby is three.'

Phil laughed, noting the woman had sidled up to him in a battered looking housecoat with her hair scraped back into a bun.

'Pardon my appearance, if you don't mind,' she said, winking. 'We don't usually get such fine visitors up here at this time of night. Where's the younger Detective who I spoke to a few days ago?'

Phil nodded. 'He's got somewhere to be but I'm the Lead Detective.'

'I thought he was too young to be the lead

Detective,' she agreed.

'What are you saying? That I'm old enough?'

She snorted quietly, snickering into her hand. 'You're probably not as old as me and I'm still pushing eight-pound monsters out of places I didn't know I could fit a bean in.'

Phil shuddered quietly at the thought then brushed it away as quickly as she had planted it there. 'Did you ever see Beth with anyone? I find it strange that she never even brought a friend or a boyfriend home to her house'

Liz retreated slightly, clearly irritated. 'I already went through this with Detective Carter. I told him I'd seen her being dropped off several times last year. I come out here to escape the racket, so I see a lot of what goes on.'

'You told Carter?' Phil felt a seethe grow within. 'Are you sure?'

'Of course, I'm sure. He asked me half a dozen times if I knew what the person looked like and if I would recognise them if I saw them again.'

'And would you?'

'No,' she answered. 'I never got a look at them. And don't ask me about the car. I couldn't tell you if it was pink, red or striped. All I knew was that it was a man and that she seemed smitten by him.'

'She told you that?'

'Not in so many words. She had a glow. She seemed tipsy one night when she got here, and I couldn't help myself, so I asked if it was her new young man. She just said it was someone she liked and that it was early days. Gave me a wink that sort of said it was a secret between her and me.'

'She clearly never told her mother.'

'Aw,' said Liz, softly. 'I get the impression they

weren't close. You know, no matter what I think of her I wouldn't wish what she's going through on anyone. And to have no family or friends come and offer support. I have five sisters and if any of my kids came to harm, they'd be kicking down the door.'

Phil smiled. 'Let's hope you never need that kind of support. What a pity she has no-one. I get the impression she doesn't accept help easily.' He turned away from Liz and saw a slight twitch in the curtain. Marilyn Phinn had clearly been listening to their conversation. He agreed with Liz. How awful it must be to be so utterly alone and to be going through this devastation with no support.

He said his goodbyes, gave one last wave to Marilyn and headed back towards his car. With every passing minute, he lost hope of ever finding Charlie Westmore alive.

56.

The house lay sinister and uninviting, a black vortex of unhappiness forever stuck in its own time. Off to the left, acres of winter wheat rose into the horizon, meeting the tip of the falling black skies at the end of the world. The fields were nothing more than marshland now, distant trees fencing it away from civilisation, but the most gruelling effect would not be known until a week after the storm had passed.

Five minutes had passed since Steve had entered the farmhouse. Donna reached into her pocket because, despite not wanting to follow Steve's instruction, long enough had passed since he'd gone into the house. She was calling in the battalion. Except, her phone was gone.

She panicked. Dug her other hand into her pockets and wrestled past her notepad, a thick fold of forgotten receipts and ran her fingers along the lining of the pocket. It wasn't there either. Donna lunged forward, running her hand under the seat and down the side of the car door. Her phone definitely wasn't to be found. She must have left it back to the office.

Fear slithering into place, Donna threw open the car door, wedged her elbow against the window and stepped into the mud. The rain quickly fell down every opening in her clothing, soaking her skin but it was nothing to the wind that pushed her back as her hair whipped her face. Why hadn't she gone with Steve anyway? She had never been a woman who would hide in the car while a man did the graft. She felt stupid now.

One foot in front of the other felt like climbing Kilimanjaro but Donna finally climbed quietly onto the wretched and broken porch. She grabbed a wooden ornament from beside the door that didn't look unlike a paddle she had once been introduced to when raiding a brothel. Another step and she was inside the house.

It was different now that she didn't have the safety or camaraderie of Phil beside her. The first thing she noticed was there was no sound. No confrontation or noisy battle that might have taken place between two male egos. Had Steve already confronted the killer? Had the killer already discovered Steve? Should she call up the stairs in case the killer was apprehended, and Steve was waiting for assistance?

A groan of the wooden floor as she moved through the house. She quickly grabbed for the bannister at the foot of the stair and clutched her chest. There was absolute darkness as far as her eyes would see. It only increased the audibility of her breath. She watched shadows pitched beneath the far lounge window, circling like vultures of death, quiet and hastened to lunge forward and pull her into their wrath. Her stomach was beginning to cramp, and she almost took comfort in the wooden object in her hand. She gave herself credit for being able to handle herself but here, she didn't know what she was facing. Her bare hands and her mind alone might not be enough to ward off the killer.

Donna began to climb the stairs, her heels knocking against each cranky beam of wood. If the killer hadn't seen them arrive, he would surely be alerted to her arrival now. No point in staying silent now. 'Steve?' How frightening the old house seemed now, more dilapidated and embroiled in darkness than it had been earlier. What once seemed a shackle now seemed a vessel to hell.

As she reached the top step, a light came into view. At the far end of the hall, the master bedroom door lay ajar with a sliver of light escaping. It wasn't enough to illuminate the hall or the other doors she would have to pass to get there. She moved slowly, aware that someone might jump out at any time. 'Steve?'

No reply.

The floorboards continued to creak, every step a musical note to alert the killer of her presence. She lifted the wooden ornament and gripped its other end with her empty hand. Then she pressed her back against the wall and continued to slide her way along. Her eyes darted back and forth between every door, watching, waiting, praying for a colleague she didn't even like to emerge from one of them.

Finally reaching the door, Donna became aware of a stench escaping the room. It was like nothing she had ever experienced in her twenty years of service, and she was almost prepared for something ungodly as she slowly pushed open the door.

As she stepped into the room, the ceiling alight in a constellation of stars from a nearby night light, it took her mere seconds to know exactly where the pungent odour was escaping from. Spread across an arrangement of lilies and daisies lay the barely recognisable remains of a putrefied body.

57.

Despite the urgency for people to get home, the foyer of Hairmyres Hospital was shockingly heaving, a collection of panicked figures racing to their cars after a twelve-hour shift and visitors now eager to shuttle themselves into the outside chaos and reach the safety of their homes.

Phil was heading in the wrong direction. He weaved through the unfocused stares and the downturned lips until he reached his destination.

Five minutes earlier, as he pulled into the hospital car park, Phil had been on the phone to the local police station, asking for more information on Kenneth Black's violent history against his late wife, as well as information on an elusive child that they were now sure must have existed. Nobody he'd spoken to recalled much about the domestic abuse accusations, nor their interactions with Kenneth. Considering what had taken place over at the farmhouse however, they were prepared to investigate a little further and call him back.

'Detective Phil Morris,' he said to the portly nurse behind the nurse station, holding up his identity badge. 'I believe you have the young man from the car explosion over in Thorntonhall.'

She smiled, revealing an uneven chain of barely white teeth and a lisp that made a hissing sound every time she spoke. 'We do. Follow me, Detective.'

He did as he was asked, following her past a trio of concrete columns until the view of a uniformed policeman came into view.

'He's in the last room at the end here. He didn't have a very comfortable night last night, I'm afraid.'

'Have you managed to get in touch with any

family?'

She shook her head. 'He won't tell us who he is. He's terrified. We told him the police would probably want to speak to him again and he became quite hysterical. I don't know what you guys did to him, but I don't think he's much for speaking to any of you.'

Phil looked in and saw that the young man inside the room was awake and was wriggling round the bed. 'How is he now?'

'He'll be due some more pain medication. He did sustain some burns to his skin but they're superficial, thankfully. He's incredibly dehydrated. I think he must have been days without even so much as a drink of water.'

Phil opened the door and followed the young man's wide-eyed gaze to the ceiling.

The nurse followed him in, fussing round the bed and fluffing the pillow behind his head. 'You're awake? It's nice to see you looking a little calmer.'

There was nothing to the room, nothing that made it remotely inviting anyway. White walls boxed a metal bed, some wires plugged up to a plastic beam and a tiny television screen that hung from the ceiling.

The man in the bed groaned, his pain etched across his face. 'I need something,' he whispered.

Phil stepped forward. 'Hello. I'm Detective Phil Morris. You probably won't remember me, but I was there when they pulled you out the car. I'm glad to see you looking a little brighter.'

The man's eyes widened some more until they were almost the shape of saucers. 'Get him out of here,' he shouted, lifting a shaky hand in protest and kicking back in the bed.

'It's okay, you've got nothing to worry about. I just need to know what you saw.'

'I'm not talking to you,' the man in the bed called. 'You're all in it together.'

The nurse stepped between them. 'Maybe this isn't the best time.'

Phil was not to be deterred though. 'There's no best time. I've got a missing girl who may or may not be dead, a potential serial killer on my streets and this young man is possibly the only living witness to the killer's identity. I'm afraid now is the only time.'

The man in the bed grabbed for the pillow. 'Get him out of here,' he shouted again, this time a little quieter than before. He looked like he might jump out of the bed any minute.

'Nobody is going to hurt you. We just need to find your kidnapper before he hurts someone else. Help us do that.'

The nurse still looked apprehensive, like she was weighing up the importance of stopping a killer against the mental well-being of her patient. 'Let me get the ward sister,' she finally said, rushing to the door and waving into the corridor.

'Do you know the person who kidnapped you?'

The young man shook his head. 'Never seen him before. He was following Charlie,' he said, finally beginning to calm. His voice still shook with deep seated nerves.

'You know Charlie?'

'I know her a little.'

Phil leaned down to the bed, holding his hands out. 'I'm just going to sit on the edge here. I'm not coming any closer. Tell me more about the person who was following her.'

The man moved back slightly, putting a little

distance between him and Phil. 'I noticed him before Charlie left the bar. He was standing in an empty doorway staring at a restaurant across the street. Just staring as if he was in a trance. Then, Charlie came out of the pub and he stepped back so she wouldn't see him. I didn't think much of it until I saw him begin to follow her.'

'Could you describe him? Would you know him if you saw him again?'

'I spent three days tied up in his car. He was the only face I saw in that time. Do you think I'll ever forget it?' He hissed, choked back a second round of tears and wiped snot on the end of his hospital gown.

'What happened after he started to follow her?'

'I followed them onto the subway and all the way to her street. Then he disappeared, or so I thought. It happened so quickly, I didn't even know he was behind me but the next thing I was being punched out and dragged into that old green car. I'm normally quite a strong guy but he was stronger than me. He managed to hold me down and get my hands behind my back. It happened so quick I didn't even think to scream before a rag was stuffed into my mouth. I was trying to get out of the boot before he locked me in.'

The man's description of events had already confirmed to Phil exactly who he was. 'Are you Tony Morgan?'

The man's eyes widened, and he peered round Phil.

'Don't worry, there's a uniformed guard out there. You're quite safe. You've also been a person of interest in this investigation. Why didn't you go back into the bar and get Garry? Or phone the police?'

'I wasn't sure at first. Garry can be a bit of a nutter so I wanted to make sure. By the time I was following them onto the subway, there wasn't any time.'

'Why didn't you try and alert Charlie?'

Tony shrugged, evidently feeling guilty now. 'I didn't want to freak her out. Garry told me about what happened to her. I thought if I just made sure she got home okay; she'd be none the wiser. The last I saw her she was going into her house. I've been hoping she got home safely.'

'She didn't.'

'I know. The nurse told me the police were already here to speak to me. I need to speak to Garry.'

'I'd prefer it if you didn't do that right now. I think we both know how Garry will react, so I think it's best you let us do our job. What do you think?'

Tony nodded.

A silence fell upon the room.

Phil looked back to the guard and gave him a light wave.

'He's one of you, you know.'

Phil spun round. 'The man who held you hostage. He's a policeman?'

Tony nodded his head again. 'Young guy, probably younger than me. Nasty looking.'

'How do you know he's a policeman?'

Tony peered at the officer again. 'He showed me his badge. Told me that if I was lucky enough to be spared, I'd never really be safe.'

'If we were to do a photo-fit, do you think you'd be able to describe him.'

Tony looked apprehensive. 'We need to find Charlie first.'

Phil rose his hand, 'Woah! Easy, tiger. I think you've got quite a bit of recuperation ahead of you. As I said to Garry, let us deal with it. We're doing everything we can.'

'The old guy?' His eyes drifted as if he were reliving something horrific.

'What about him?'

'I could hear him, smell the smoke, feel the flames burning in that car. I've never heard or smelt anything like it.'

'Do you know who he was?'

'I only saw him for a second. He was drunk, I think. Older than you, probably.'

Another confirmation to Phil that Kenneth Black had been the body in the front of the car. They just needed to await official confirmation.

'We believe that the car was probably used to transport Charlie. Did you hear her? Did you hear him speak to her? Her speak to him?'

'Not a thing,' answered Tony. I tried to listen because there was nothing else to do. I don't think there was anybody else in that car. If there was, they didn't make a sound.'

That made sense to Phil. Charlie had probably been given the same sedative as the other girls.

'He'll have killed her by now.'

Phil shook his head. 'I don't think so. That's not how he works. There's still a chance.' He heard the words coming out of his mouth, the offer of hope that he no longer felt himself. What else could he say. It had been the motto of himself and anyone who worked with him that while there was no news, there was hope. They would never give up until they found her.

Tony's eyes tightened. 'You really believe I'm safe with that officer out there?'

'I think you were just in the wrong place at the wrong time. I don't think this killer has any need for you. You've seen his face. That's the only thing that might pose a threat. That's why I'm going to insist that officer stays with you until we catch him.'

Tony didn't look convinced.

Phil leaned towards him. 'I promise you that nothing bad is going to happen.'

The man looked round the room as if fearing that he was being watched or monitored. He rubbed the ligature marks and the surrounding bruises on his wrists and smirked. 'I hope you're right because I don't fancy a second go with this maniac. He might not be so generous next time.'

58.

The smell had quickly settled in her nostrils, but it was the vision of the rotten corpse that would really give Donna sleepless nights. In her twenty years of policing she had seen enough dead bodies to fill a cemetery, but this was new even for her. It had been fashioned across the floor as if being paraded on a float. The anatomy was long gone but Donna had seen a few decomposed bodies and suspected that the shortness of the waist bones meant the remains were probably female.

She turned away when she could no longer stand to stare at it. She looked round the room and noted that nothing much else seemed disturbed since their earlier visit. It begged the question of who the remains belonged to? Donna didn't have time to investigate that now. Somewhere in this house, she suspected Steve must be hurt. Why else had he disappeared? She was about to turn away when she heard any almighty clatter from downstairs. Now she knew she wasn't alone.

Donna lunged for the door, still gripping onto the wooden object in her hand and made her way to the top of the stairs. The clattering was louder now. The confrontation she had expected upon arrival must be taking place now. She reached the top of the stairs. 'Steve?'

'Hurry, Donna. He's getting away.'

Donna leapt down the stairs, taking two at a time and made her way into the lounge. Steve was gone. The only noise now was the banging of some contraption from the far side of the lounge. She moved forward, waving the object in her hand at her side. If someone jumped out on her, she would be ready. Finally, she arrived to find the banging noise was coming from the back door which was placed at the end of the old kitchen.

The outer door, an old mesh contraption hung together within an iron frame, battered against the house as lightning cracked across the sky. If there was one thing that gave Donna the shivers, it was thunder and lightning. Yet, she couldn't let Steve face the killer himself. She darted out onto the back porch and as another round of lightning passed across the sky, it illuminated the vision of Steve's head disappearing into the crops.

As she headed in the same direction, Donna recalled the horrific expression on the faces of the first two victims. Even if they were close to finding Charlie, Donna now feared there was little chance that the girl would still be alive. The other girls were dead in less than twenty-four hours. The temperatures had dipped somewhat since then. Donna didn't believe in miracles. She moved into the dead shrubs amongst the once promising crops.

Donna was glad of the tiny amount of light from the partial moon. At least she wasn't in complete darkness as she headed after Steve and the killer. The further she went, the duller the light from the partially concealed moon transpired to be. There was little chance of avoiding the pull of the marshes, so Donna took the hits wherever they landed. Rainwater had already poured in through the gaps in her shoes, the hem of her trousers and soaked through to her socks. The walk to the centre of the crops felt long and arduous, her hair clinging to her face, her shoulders heavy from the weight of the downpour and all that she had endured recently.

The storm continued, ferocious and unrelenting

as she finally reached the centre of the crops. She had long lost Steve, frightened to call out for him just in case she gave the killer the opportunity to find her before she found him.

The wind caught her dead on the face when she emerged from inside the mask of the crops. Now she was completely exposed. That didn't concern Donna. What immediately caught her attention was the massive pit barrelled deep into the earth at the heart of the land. Without another thought for her own safety, she thrust forward until she reached the end of the giant pit and peered over. She could no longer keep herself from calling out. 'Charlie?'

The pit was empty.

Donna stood, wiping the wet away from her reddening face. Under the pressure of expectation, the stillness caught her square in the chest, and she had to take a deep breath just to focus herself.

Something moved. Or someone.

Donna's eye twitched. She looked round herself, wondering where Steve could be. Was he still in pursuit of the killer? Had he found him yet? Would any of them get out of here alive? Was the killer watching her now? The thought caused her to shudder. 'Hello?'

A sound from below.

There was definite movement. A patch of earth shifted and suddenly it looked as if the ground was opening. Enough moonlight dropped that Donna set her eyes upon the battered features of a young woman, naked and hunched as she climbed out of the hole in the earth.

'Help me,' cried the girl, her voice almost inaudible behind the howl of the wind.

Donna threw the wooden ornament to the

ground, her eyes widened, and she leapt into action. ‘Charlie?’

‘Help me,’ the girl said again, her voice cracking now as she realised, someone had finally found her.

59.

Phil was about to ring Donna when his mobile phone sprang to life. They'd been barking up the wrong tree the whole time. Tony hadn't disappeared because he'd taken Charlie, he'd disappeared because he'd tried to protect her. The theory that Tony might be Kenneth's stepson had just flown out the window. If it wasn't Tony, then who?

'Phil Morris?'

The voice at the other end was the same voice he'd spoken to a few minutes earlier. 'Hello, Phil. It's Brian Worsley here. I spoke to you a few minutes ago about the investigation into the death of Kenneth Black.'

'Thanks for calling me back. 'Did you find anything?'

'In a way,' muttered the other Detective. 'You were exactly right about him having a son, well a stepson anyway. He never adopted the boy which is why it hasn't really flagged up. He was married to the boy's mother, Susan.'

'I read all about her,' said Phil, thinking aloud. 'She pressed charges against him several times, didn't she?'

'And always dropped them again,' said Worsley. 'That's why we were never able to convict the scumbag.' He paused for a second. 'Sorry, I shouldn't speak ill of the dead.'

'If it's even him that's dead,' mused Phil, frustrated by how much time had been wasted on the several wild goose chases presented to them.

'We're still waiting on an identification. Unfortunately, being burned to death is very inconvenient when you're trying to piece together an identity in a timeous manner.'

Phil chuckled. 'Okay, so I know the wife took her own life. What about the stepson, do we know where he is?'

'In all honesty, if it hadn't been for a single solitary referral to social work, we probably wouldn't have known there was a stepson. There's no mention of him in any of his charge sheets.'

'What was the social work referral for then?'

Worsley went silent, the only audible sound in the handset coming from his obvious fumbling with paperwork. 'I've got it here. It was after the wife's death. The son made some startling accusations against Black, saying he was abusive to him. At that time, it was considered a family matter, so it was referred to social work.

'Shocking,' said Phil, already feeling apologetic for another failure in the system. 'What happened? Was he arrested?'

'There was no foundation to it,' said Worsley. 'The boy claimed that he regularly beat him, but the only mark on his body was from an accident that he previously claimed happened at school. Black said he was a liar. The boy also claimed that he'd been lowered into the well and left there to die for four days. Social workers could find no evidence that this ever happened and had to conclude that Black was right, the boy was a liar who was confused and upset about his mother's death.'

'Kenneth Black probably drove his wife to her suicide. Yet, nobody could find any basis for this boy's claims. What the hell was going on with this family? What was going on with social work, for Christ's sake?'

'He would probably be removed and placed in

care now,' said Worsley.

'Too late to care,' snapped Phil. 'He's now out killing women from my city, so you'll forgive me if I'm not feeling particularly guilty that he had a crap childhood on account of someone's negligence.'

'It's unfortunate,' agreed Worsley.

'Unfortunate is not the word I'd use. Anyway, have you got a name and address for him?'

The man fumbled some more, exhaling loudly. A moment later, he read aloud the name and last known address for Kenneth Black's stepson. Phil recoiled as he stopped running his pen across the page. He disconnected without saying goodbye to Worsley and quickly scrolled through his call list. The second last number that phoned him was Donna. So, he pressed on her name and watched her photo flash across his screen. She'd be at the farmhouse by now. He only hoped it wasn't too late.

A second later the familiar voice of a man came through the handset. 'Hello, Mister Morris. Do you know where your fiancé is right now?'

60.

'Charlie, sweetheart. I'm going to find a way to get you out of there. I need you to stay silent and calm for now. Do you understand?' Donna continued to stare into the pit, her mind conjuring up solutions that didn't seem that reachable.

The girl shook her head, staring up through slits at the centre of her blistered eyelids.

Donna's heart was beating faster than she knew possible as she headed towards the barren trees at the back of the pit. She knew she had to act fast because Steve couldn't stave off the killer forever. Wherever they were, that maniac was coming for Charlie. Donna didn't have a minute to spare. There was no time for her not to be proactive. Still, her terror remained.

Donna stood, looked round herself and then weaved through the trees. Finally, she found what she was looking for. Pressed up against the back of the largest bark was a twenty-foot ladder. Donna raced to it, thinking nothing of how heavy it might be. No time to be weak now, she thought to herself.

A crack stopped her in her tracks. Was someone watching?

Donna stumbled slightly, grabbing for a nearby fence only to find a piece of barbed wire catching on her hand. She almost let out a scream, then threw the bloody hand to her mouth.

She found herself feeling how she suspected those girls must have felt when they realised they were caught in someone's lair. No time to think of that now though. Donna grabbed for the wooden ladder and dragged it quickly back to the pit. When she looked down, she could see Charlie hunched over with her arms wrapped round her breasts. 'Charlie, sweetheart. I'm going to lower down the ladder so you're able to climb up to me. I need you to do it quickly. I know you're probably unable to see much so I'm going to guide you okay.'

'Don't let him kill me,' shrieked the girl.

Donna smiled. 'It's alright, Charlie. I'll keep you safe.' Right now, Donna didn't know how much of that promise she could keep.

Charlie shook her head, becoming more frantic as she began to climb the steps of the ladder.

'You have nothing to be frightened of,' lied Donna. 'I'm right here. Detective Carter is with me. We're going to get you to safety.' Donna smiled at her, desperately beckoning, her silent urge for Charlie to hurry beginning to spread through her.

'Steve's with you?'

Donna smiled, wondering if Steve had been the magic word. She looked back down and saw that Charlie now clung to the ladder and seemed to have stopped moving. 'Quick, Charlie. You've not got many more to go.' She lay down on her breast and stretched her hand out.

Charlie was moving quicker now. With only a few more steps to go, she was grabbing frantically for every step until she was able to reach out and touch Donna's hand.

Donna nodded reassuringly, the urge to scream with happiness buried beneath her knowledge that any minute now they could both be killed.

Charlie finally stepped onto land as Donna took off her jacket and wrapped it round Charlie's shoulders. Her lips were trembling as the rest of her body began to shake violently. She looked as if she was trying to say something, but the words wouldn't come.

'Come on, Charlie. We've got to find Steve quickly and get out of here.'

Another rustling from the crops, this time louder. Not the gentle wrestling against the wind but the obvious arrival of another person.

Donna grabbed for the wooden paddle on the ground and stepped in front of Charlie. 'Don't move, Charlie. Stay behind me.'

A moment later, a dark figure emerged from behind the shield of the centre crops.

Charlie gasped in horror.

Donna let out a sigh of relief. 'Steve? Thank god.'

Steve lifted his eyes and scowled. 'Charlie Farley. You're still alive. You've really surpassed all of my expectations.'

61.

Phil dialed his chief's number, knowing all too well that the old crank would be doubly cranky at this time of night. Roger Burns, former veteran and new Chief of police was not a man who liked to have his evenings interrupted.

The phone rang twice and then the gruff East Coast voice sprang through. 'This better be good.'

'Chief, I need a warrant to search Steve Carter's home.' He pulled the car over the side of the road.

'What are you talking about? Carter's one of us. Why do you need to search his house?'

'He's the killer, chief. I think he's only joined the force to enable him to kill those women undetected. What better way to stay ahead of the game?'

'Are you sure? You know he's an army boy. Fought for queen and country before coming to us.'

Phil had always known it would be a hard sell. The chief had taken Carter in as one of his own, impressed by his unblemished his record as well as his time in Afghanistan. They had all been as equally stupid.

'I'm sure.'

'Well, being a veteran is not a license to kill on home soil.'

Phil wanted to lose it. There was nowhere in the world that should permit license to kill. Not home soil, not anywhere else. 'That's right, chief,' he said, bottling the urge to enter a war of words.

'Okay,' said Burns. 'I'll get it sorted. Have you got him in custody?'

'Not yet,' replied Phil, his mind turning back to Kate. She would be his next port of call. 'We need to act quickly, Chief.

No more words were spoken. The phone was disconnected.

62.

It hadn't been his plan to kill Kenneth Black. Steve only wanted to come home, to claim back what was his. He expected a confrontation, but the old man would be no match for him now. Three years in the armed forces, another ten preparing for his act of vengeance and he wanted his stepfather to know what was born of his cruelty.

He had rather enjoyed the sound of Kenneth screaming as the flames burned up his body. Elation had quickly fuelled him, but he soon found that it floundered to make way for the memory of his fear. Kenneth doesn't have that power now but, once upon a time he was all Steve feared. A father like no other, a monster that has penetrated his mind for too many years.

He's just made the call to Phil. He expects that Phil will have sprung into action, made the jolly home so he can save his beloved betrothed. If only he knew how close to death Kate was, he'd be forever grateful that tonight's little rouse was nothing more than a ploy to get him out of the way. For now.

He feels his lips squaring back to reveal his teeth. A jaguar in human form, he rather enjoys the knowledge that Donna finally gets to be vindicated in her hatred of him. Didn't she always know he was bad? Hadn't she tried to tell everyone? Nobody believed her. Not that she could even imagine the extent of how bad he is. Maybe he'll tell her how much he respects her instincts. In those final moments, as he garrottes the life out of her and reveals that she's his substitute number four, he might just give her that last crumb.

His thoughts turn to Charlie. She should be dead

now. She thinks he doesn't know she tricked him. That's what makes it so enjoyable. How could she ever think she was clever enough to outsmart him? Even at her best, she would never have gotten the better of him. The enjoyment of her has passed, his patience expired. He'll no longer wait for her to die at the hands of the storm. She'll know soon what it's like to really be violated. Johnny McCabe is small change compared to him.

A shiver of excitement.

As the wooden paddle in her hand swings towards his face, he jumps back. It'll take more than a smack to the head for her to better him. He leaps forward, knocks the paddle to the ground and grabs for her arm. She surprises him though by swinging her leg at his knee and knocking his balance away.

Steve drops.

It's only for a second but its long enough to facilitate her escape. She grabs Charlie's muddy hand and drags her away.

She is running. Disappearing into the crops and doing exactly what he knew she would. The car will be her first stop. Only, the car is gone. He's ensured that by hiding her obvious escape mode, double insuring himself by stabbing a knife into the tyres. In the likely event that the two of them get free of his clutches, it won't be on those four wheels.

He is following them now, deepening into the crops until the wind only howls above him. His mind turns to the real number four, the incomparable beauty that brought her to his attention in the first place. Her death would have driven a stake into Phil's heart. Two destructions for the price of one. Wouldn't that be something, the smug arrogance of his senior wiped out in one fell swoop? Kate Mulgrew will probably never know how lucky she just got.

63.

The car was gone. As the dense cold continued to batter at Donna, her hair still matted to her face, she tried not to give into her panic. She needed Charlie to feel safe. She would worry about herself later.

For a moment, as they stopped and stared at the house, Donna knew she couldn't take Charlie there. He was counting on them returning there. It was why he had taken the car out of sight so that they had no other option but to go back into the house and seek shelter there. If Charlie was to see that body, Donna was afraid it might be just enough to send her over the edge. Or end her.

Donna wanted to take a moment to feel rage. Rage that she had been right all along. Why had nobody trusted her instincts? Not even she could have imagined just how evil he was, but the manipulation was as clear as daylight to her. She turned back and saw the wind turbine rotate at twice the normal speed, the clattering echoing through the night air. It only reminded her that she was on his land and that he knew every nook and cranny. There would be nowhere to hide.

'Come on,' she finally said. Donna grabbed Charlie's hand again, but Charlie looked as if she just wanted to lay down and die. 'Charlie, now's not the time to give up. God knows how you done it, girl but you survived where two other girls didn't. You're alive.'

Charlie continued to shiver, her blazing eyes blinking as if they were batting away long serving tears. 'He'll find us.'

'You know what, sweetheart? You're right. We've got nowhere to go until the cavalry arrives.

That's why we have to be prepared.'

Steve hollered their names from inside the crops, taunting them as he closed the gap.

Donna took another glance at the house. She was not going back in there. Finally, she grabbed at Charlie again and pulled her towards the barn. Back out in the open, they had to throttle through the wind and rain as storm Maggie met them square in the chest. As they reached the barn, the doors swung open and thumped against the outer wall. 'Come on, let's get in here.'

She pulled the doors closed behind her and grabbed for a small torch that sat on a nearby shelf. As she switched it on and searched the back end of the barn, she ran towards a raincoat that hung on a nearby hook. 'Here, Charlie. Get this on. It'll at least keep you dry if we have to run again.'

Outside, Steve emerged from the crops, cackling and howling at the sky. He turned towards the house.

'Phil will be on his way but for now we need to try and ward him off as long as we can.' Donna switched off the torch and pushed Charlie under one of the large square wall shelves. 'He thinks we've gone to the house.'

'Why didn't we?' Charlie was stuttering, her voice barely more than a throaty whisper.

'You don't want to see what's in that house. We've bought ourselves some time here. Just stay hidden under here and whatever you do, don't come out unless I tell you to.'

'Okay,' said the girl, pulling back until she was completely concealed by the shelf above.

Donna moved back towards the door so she could watch through the window. As she stared at the house, her eyes darting back and forth, she watched for any sign that he was coming back out. She stayed there for untold minutes. The whole time she was hoping he'd fall through a hole in the floor and break his neck. She knew she wouldn't get that lucky.

'Donna?'

'Yes, sweetheart,' she replied, turning back to see Charlie poke her head out of the square unit.

Charlie lifted her hand and pointed. 'Someone's there.'

Donna spun round, saw Steve staring from the other side of the barn door and let out a scream.

He threw it open, knocking Donna to the ground and pounding down on her.

The wind threw the doors open again, this time more violently.

Charlie clamoured out from under the unit and moved round the barn, passing an army of garden tools until she was as far from Steve as she could get.

Steve wasn't interested in her now. He had his hand round Donna's throat and was pushing her against the wall. 'I'm going to enjoy this.'

Donna felt the pressure against her windpipe. She dug her fingernails into his skin, trying to force him to let go. Meanwhile, the wind continued to pound violently at the barn, the rain washing down the grime and dirt from its outer walls.

'Let her go,' said a voice from behind.

Donna tried to catch a breath. Even though she couldn't quite get it, she was still relieved to see Phil storm into the barn and throw a punch at the side of Steve's head.

Steve let go of Donna just in time for her to fall to the ground and grab for her throat. He grabbed for a pitchfork that hung from the barn wall and swung it at Phil. Phil threw himself to the ground and then kicked his leg out just in time to catch Steve in the groin.

The pitchfork fell to the ground.

Phil was about to jump to his feet when lightning crashed across the sky and struck down on the roof of the barn. A hole blew through the wooden slats causing rubble to come crashing down on the corner of the barn.

'Charlie?' Donna screamed and ran towards it.

As another collection of logs suddenly fell, Phil pulled her back. 'Don't. You'll get bloody killed.'

As she stared at the rubble now building on the ground, she saw Steve stand and make a dash for the door. 'Phil,' she screamed. 'He's getting away.'

Phil took to his feet. 'Stay here,' he called as he trampled out into the rain.

Donna had no intention of staying put for a second time. She followed him outside and noted that Steve had completely disappeared. 'Where is he?'

Phil stared across the land, eyeing the deserted house and the rotating turbine, the wavering crops and the barren trees. Then he eyed the inside of the barn. ''The bridge is closed. Besides, he wants to finish this,' said Phil. 'He's not going anywhere.'

64.

The dam finally broke just after nine p.m. The rain had fallen so heavily that the waters had risen and formed a stream at either side of the bridge that led into Blackwood Farm. The bridge itself had become damaged as the storm caused one side to cave in and create a barrier that would not be easy to cross. The roads on either side were also flooded so any dip in the road or swerve now lay at the bottom of rising sewers.

Sargent Brian Worsley had unwillingly agreed he would return to the land, despite his reservations about putting his own staff in jeopardy. He watched from quarter of a mile up the road as a murky waterfall heeled any opportunity they might have once had of safe passage. There was no way they were getting to the farmhouse now. Which meant a deranged killer was now up there with two people at his mercy.

'Damn Phil Morris for bringing this to our doorstep.'

'That's a bit unfair, Sarge.' Police Constable Scott Edwards, ever the voice of reason reversed back so he could turn in a different direction. 'After all, Steve Carter owns that land.'

'Indeed,' huffed McGregor. 'Anyway, there's no way we can get there now. We'll need to hit the back roads and do a full circle. I don't fancy the two young woman's chances against him.'

'You speak as if you know him, Sarge.'

Worsley tracked his thoughts back fourteen years. 'I met him once. Right before he disappeared. He made some pretty wild accusations against Kenneth Black.'

'What kind of accusations?'

'Abuse. You know the sort. Not the kind of thing we wanted here. Kenneth always had a wild temper and he was known to like a drink or two. I think it's fair to say he only married Carter's mother to get his hands on her fortune.'

Edwards frowned. 'She was rich?'

'Land rich probably. I don't think she had two shillings to rub together. In fact, I'd say she probably only married him because he was a decent farm hand and she hoped he'd manage to restore the land to its former glory. It was her father's farm, you see.'

'What were the accusations. He didn't...?' His voice trailed off, as if he couldn't bear to say the words aloud.

'I never heard anything like that,' replied Worsley. 'Physical abuse, mental torture and even claims of imprisonment against his will.'

'He locked him up?'

'According to little Steve, Black once lowered him into the well at the back of their farmhouse and left him there for days.'

'Why wasn't he arrested?'

'No proof. Most people didn't believe it happened. He claimed he was starved and dehydrated. There was no evidence that he was suffering malnutrition or dehydration. By all accounts, the kid seemed pretty disturbed.'

Edwards sighed. 'Then how the fuck did he get into the academy?'

'That's the beauty of a sociopath. They are so convincing, even they believe their own lies. Nobody knew what became of him after he upped and left the farmhouse. He is known as Steve Carter now, taking his mother's maiden name. Back then, he was known as Steven Black.'

'He changed his identity?'

'Not really. He took back his own identity, but it just goes to show that if a person wants to disappear, it's really not that difficult.'

'I don't understand it. If he's managed to build a life for himself, getting into the force and everything, then why go back to exact revenge on Black? And why involve other people?'

'Who knows,' replied Worsley. 'If we don't get there pretty damn quick though, I suspect we'll have another two bodies on our hands.'

65.

'You help Charlie, I'm going after him.'

Phil and Donna were stranded at Blackwood Farm. He had just delivered the bad news about the bridge into the farm caving in. It meant nobody was getting in and they were certainly not getting out.

Donna ran towards the rubble at the far end of the barn whilst Phil made his way out into the wild. 'Carter?' His voice rose up to meet the falling gales as he hunkered towards the house.

Once inside, he stormed through the lounge and into the hallway. If Steve truly wanted to finish this, where better than home turf. He would know every corner of the land, every place to hide and every single tool that he could use on them. Phil knew they were at a disadvantage. It didn't deter him.

'Come on, Steve. Don't keep me waiting. You want to kill us all, let's have it.'

No sound.

'You wanted to use Kate to keep me away. Well, it didn't work. I know exactly where my fiancé is. You can't be standing outside our house watching someone who isn't even there.'

Nothing.

'How many more. Huh?' Phil was screaming now, his sodden clothes clinging to his skin, his greying hair dripping sprays of water every time he moved.

The house remained in perfect silence, a place that had only every known evil and violence. Phil continued to climb the stairs, each one creaking beneath him and even he suddenly knew what it was to feel afraid.

'This won't end if you're going to hide away,' he

called. 'I know what Black did to you. We all know now. You blame him for your mother dying?'

Something fluttered in the distance. In Phil's mind, a bat. Probably nothing quite as dark or sinister.

'People don't force people into committing suicide.'

Still nothing.

Phil was starting to wonder if Steve had returned home or had perhaps fled. Why wasn't he reacting? Perhaps he had patience that Phil simply couldn't appreciate. After all, he didn't operate like a normal man. All these years of plotting, waiting and preparing himself for the perfect storm.

'I'm leaving now,' Phil finally said. Was that what Steve was waiting to hear?

Phil turned his back, walked back towards the stairs and began to descend. Every step he took, every breath in and out, Phil waited to be attacked. He finally arrived on the ground floor and took a deep breath.

66.

Donna felt his breath on the back of her neck.

'It looks like he abandoned you, after all,' said Steve.

She swung round, stared him squarely in the face and hissed. 'Yet, he's still a hundred times the man you'll ever be.'

He laughed. 'Is that supposed to upset me. That the love of your life is a better man than me.' He leaned forward. 'Then why is he screwing somebody else?'

She spat. 'Only a mind like yours would go there. Is that really what this is all about for you? That nobody wants to fuck you. Is kidnapping them the only way you can get your kicks?'

His face changed slightly.

'Who does the body belong to up there?'

He shook his head violently.

'Is that your mother? Are you hoping that if you kill enough women, she'll come back to life?'

'Don't be stupid,' he roared. 'People don't come back to life.

She leaned forward and smiled. 'No, they don't.'

He grabbed her throat and pushed her down a little. 'You think you're a match for me? You think I wont just snap your neck and leave those dear little twins with your demented old mother? You're not exactly in the league of the first three, but Kate couldn't quite make it. You'll do.'

The realisation felt like a punch in the face. He had a full selection planned out. 'Why those girls?' Her neck was beginning to ache, as was the arch in her back.

'Why not?'

'If you're going to kill me, at least tell me why?'

'Don't try and put me off. You're not buying time. We don't have time for your crap.' He pulled her away, still clutching at her neck.

Donna felt herself being almost dragged and wanted to scream. She wouldn't give him the satisfaction. Pride before the fall.

They were outside now, him dragging her round the side of the barn.

'You want to know why four?'

'Four?'

'The number of women I planned to kill. There was a reason for it.'

Donna tried to punch at him, pull herself away but his grip was too strong.

'Four days I spent down that well.' He pointed at the brick monument only a few yards away. 'I was lucky to survive. So much so that nobody believed I could have been down there that amount of time. I reckon that nobody could realistically survive it for more than a day. So, I needed four women to know what four days would feel like.'

As she tumbled towards the well, she finally managed to free his grip.

'Why punish women for what a man did to you?'

He laughed, almost as if the sex of his victims barely mattered. 'I could have chosen men, maybe Phil could have been my victim number four. Maybe he still can. Do you think you can run fast enough to escape me?'

She wasn't even going to try. She'd no more give him the satisfaction of seeing her run than scream. 'You're really quite sure that you'd get the better of him. You manipulated people into trusting you and then came up behind them. You're no match for Phil or any other man I know.'

His face twisted into rage and he pushed forward so quickly that she wasn't expecting it.

Donna fell to the ground, twisting her wrist and letting out a shallow yelp. A deep puddle splashed up onto her face and she prepared herself for him to pound down on her.

Instead, she turned just in time to see a pitchfork hit against the side of Steve's head as he rolled to the ground and let out an angry roar.

Donna's eyes followed the metal contraption until she found herself staring into the raging eyes of the person holding it.

'I'm finishing this tonight.'

67.

So, Steve hadn't returned to the house. Which was a surprise to Phil. He now returned to the raging elements and hurtled towards the barn. Halfway there he suddenly heard Steve screaming. They were behind the barn.

He began to run, frightened that Donna would either unleash her fury or become Steve's fourth victim. 'Donna?'

Sirens wailed into the distance, their back up finally finding a way around the flooding to come and assist.

Phil continued towards the side of the barn, just in time to see Donna push to her feet and move towards Steve.

To their right, Steve was eyeing something that wasn't quite visible to Phil yet. He was talking animatedly but no sound could be heard because storm Maggie now howled so loud that there was no cutting through her sound at this distance.

Finally, Phil arrived and found Charlie standing with a pitchfork in her hand.

She was aiming the metal contraption straight at Steve's chest.

'Move, over there. Quick!'

Steve held his hands up, snickered slightly and nodded. 'Charlie Farley, you're not going to use that. Let's be serious.'

'Don't call me that. I hated it even when I didn't know you were a psycho.' Her eyes still looked as if they might burst into flames any minute, but it was nothing to the rage that lay behind them.

'Charlie, put that down.' Phil moved to the side of her. 'This isn't just about you. There's two other young woman who deserve justice. Killing him isn't going to achieve that.'

'I don't care,' she said.

'If I believed that, I'd walk away and let you do whatever you wanted to do. He doesn't deserve to live, but you don't deserve to live the rest of your life as someone who has taken a life.'

She wiped her cheek.

'Do you think you'll sleep any better knowing that you've killed someone?'

She snorted. 'I'll sleep better knowing there's one less like him on the streets.'

'He's already murdered three people and attempted to kill you. He's not walking anywhere.'

Charlie turned her head slightly, evidently wavering over what Phil was saying.

Steve suddenly lunged forward, knocking the pitchfork from her hand and discombobulating her just long enough to grab her and pull her to the well. He now had her bent over the edge of the bricks.

Charlie screamed. 'You should have let me kill him when I had the chance,' she wailed.

'Don't come any closer or I'll break her neck and drop her in there,' ordered Steve.

The sirens were now much closer.

'Don't do it. You've got nothing left to gain,' said Phil. He saw from the side of his eye that Donna was slipping into his vision and now had the pitchfork in her hands.

'It'll make me feel one step closer to my goal. Three dead, only one to go.' He yanked Charlie's head back.

'You'll still have failed,' smirked Phil.

'Maybe. Or maybe Donna and Kate won't feel so safe in their little bubbles. Or maybe I'll just wait until I'm in prison and find some pretty little prison guard.'

With the mention of her name, Donna lunged forward, dug the pitchfork into his chest as he let go of Charlie.

Charlie pulled away, threw herself out of harm's way and screamed.

Steve's eyes darted up, blood seeping from six different wound sites in his chest. He hurtled backwards, grabbed for the side of the well and spat a blood clot from his lips.

Phil darted forward, throwing out his hand to give Steve a final lifeline.

The man gargled more blood in his mouth, drew back his lips and revealed a set of smiling red teeth. Then he rolled over the edge of the well, his body flying to his death and he let out one last scream before he hit the stone floor at the bottom of the old dry well.

Donna dropped the pitchfork and threw her hands to her shocked face.

Phil quickly rushed to her side and grabbed her into his arms. 'You did the only thing you could do.'

Charlie moved, reached for the pitchfork now lying on the ground and ran her hands along the edge.

'Charlie, don't touch that,' said Phil, letting go of Donna.

She continued to run her hands along the edge. She looked up at Donna, defiantly. Then she threw the pitchfork into the well. 'If anybody asks what happened, you tell them I dug that contraption right into the bastard's chest.' Then she turned, closing the rain mac across her breasts and walked towards the arriving police vehicles.

68.

Phil sat at his desk, satisfied that storm Maggie had died along with Steve Carter. Once his reign of terror was ended, Maggie seemed to be able to rest. The city was now rebuilding itself, a sense of neighbourhood and community restored as one rushed to help another following Maggie's destruction.

'It was so simple, I didn't even think of it,' said Phil. 'They found traces of weed killer on Michelle and Beth's skin, but I wasn't focused on that because they were probably rolling round in those pits for hours.'

'The tarpaulin?'

'We found over three hundred meters of it at his flat. I think he laid it out from the car to the side of the pit, meaning that the car didn't have to come anywhere near the pit. We went back and found that there were tyre marks approximately two hundred meters away from the pit we found Beth in. It's also why we didn't find any of his footprints. We also found Michelle, Beth and Charlie's DNA in his wheelie bin. I suspect that's what he used to drop them into the pit without having to go down there himself.'

'He quite literally treated them like rubbish,' said Donna. 'What about the hair we found on Beth?'

'Carrie told me he made two visits to the mortuary after Beth's body was found. She didn't question it because, why would she? If he was part of the investigating team, it wouldn't be unheard of for him to visit. I think he planted the hair then. I also think it's why he deliberately contaminated the site where Beth was found.'

'What do you mean?' Donna looked perplexed.

'Maybe he thought he'd mucked it up. Perhaps he figured that if he'd left any of his own DNA there, he'd cover his tracks by accidently deliberately screwing it up in plain sight.'

'You have to wonder what kind of mind even thinks up what he plotted.'

'The same one that would dig his own mother's body up just to put the frighteners up someone.' Phil grabbed for the picture that lay on his desk, the one of Michelle Evans that had been taken in a bar. 'The bar this was taken in is called 'The Anchor'. I spoke to some of the staff there last night and they remembered Michelle going in there a few times with a man. I showed them the picture of Steve and they think it was him, though only one of them seemed sure. It was well over a year ago, so the CCTV from that time is long gone.'

'He was grooming them towards this. That's why he manipulated them into staying silent about their relationship.'

'Except Charlie. They never had a sexual relationship. He manipulated her in a different way, befriending her so she would feel safe, encouraged her to change her name and made her feel that she could turn to him. He made her feel he was her only friend in Glasgow.'

'Did they find the object he used to brand them? I still wonder how he was able to do that without leaving a single shred of evidence.'

'Probably much the same way that he got them in there in the first place. The tarpaulin hides a multitude of sins. If you watch back some of the CCTV, you'll see that on his visits to the site after their deaths, there's a ladder on the top of the car. He wouldn't have to step into the pit, only climb down far enough to hold the poker to their faces.' Phil clicked on the screen to reveal a poker where a metal star had been welded on to the end. 'It wouldn't have taken much to have it adjusted. He probably done it at home.'

'I hope he rots in hell,' hissed Donna.

Phil nodded in agreement. 'Hell's too good for him.'

'Maybe they should have left him down in that well then. No point wasting a good casket on him.'

Phil snickered. 'Enough,' he ordered. 'I'll be speaking to Michelle's mum on the phone later. She sent an email with all the questions, half of which I still don't have any answers to. The woman is entitled to closure.'

'Do you want me to be there?'

'I don't think it matters who is there. How do you soft pedal that her daughter will never come home again. If you want to come in, then you're welcome. If I were you, I'd take the free out while its on offer. You're not getting it with Marilyn Phinn when I go and speak to her tonight.'

'I'm going to see Charlie tonight. She's being kept in hospital for a few more days and I think her brother is driving her up the wall.'

'That's convenient,' teased Phil. 'I'll take someone else to speak to Marilyn.'

'Are you sure?'

'I'm sure. Anyway, you're going to be late,' he said, ushering her out the door.

Donna smiled. 'I'm as nervous as hell. I hope I'm doing the right thing.'

Phil stood and grabbed her hands. 'You are doing the right thing for you and for your mum. It's a nice home. They'll take good care of her.'

A tear appeared in Donna's right eye. 'It's

breaking my blood heart.' She snorted back a full geyser of tears.

'I know.' He put his arms round her and gave her a tight hug. 'Old mammy would understand.'

Donna blubbered and nodded when she was no longer able to speak. Without another word, she pulled away and quickly departed.

Phil turned back and looked at the picture of Michelle Evans and Beth Phinn. He felt the sinking of his gut as he realised, he hadn't done right by then. He hadn't gotten them justice and he hadn't brought them back to life. The only thing he could do was deliver closure to their mothers. Even that didn't feel enough. He tenderly tucked their picture away and resisted the urge to punch the computer screen in when Steve Carter's face appeared on it. He switched the laptop off and drew his breath in. It was time to make that phone call.

69.

Five months later

Nobody had warned Kate Mulgrew that planning a wedding would almost send her over the edge. The night before the big event, rather than relaxing at the spa that Phil had arranged for her, Donna and Charlie, she was meeting with the celebrant for a run-through of her vows and a second-by-second play out of her walk down the aisle. Any notion that it would be an improvised affair was long abandoned once she realised her celebrant wasn't just going to marry her but also control every element of her day and direct her like she was a god damn film star.

Still, Kate was deliriously happy. She had waited two years for this moment. Phil had waited even longer. She stared into the mirror, her brown hair twisted back into a set of curls atop her hair and the train of the dress sparkling with a trail of diamantes. If it hadn't been her own image staring back at her, she might have whooshed at how stunning the whole thing looked.

Charlie walked to her side. 'Breath-taking,' she muttered. 'You know, if he doesn't already know he's punching above his weight, we'll soon let him know.'

Donna laughed. 'Exactly. And if he doesn't marry you, we will.'

Laughter filled the room.

'I can't believe it's finally here,' sighed Kate, an unwitting tear appearing at the centre of her eye. 'I'm so glad you two are at my side. I couldn't ask for better friends.'

Donna and Charlie both leaned in and hugged her at the same time.

Donna snickered. 'I wouldn't wear a dress for

anyone else. And if you tell anyone that I cried, I'm coming after you as soon as the honeymoon is over.'

Kate lifted her arms and pulled them both to her. 'Your secret's safe with us. Are you ready?'

'Born ready. Are you?'

Kate's lips upturned until her face was almost aching. She nodded excitedly and grabbed for the bouquet.

The haunting sound of Enya's 'Only Time' filled the hall as Kate followed her two bridesmaids down a wooden staircase. The brass banister slipped by in her sweaty hands. Her smile spread once more when she saw Harry at the bottom of the stairs awaiting her. 'You look handsome,' she said as she approached, impressed by just how well he wore the grey tuxedo.

'Not as handsome as you,' he replied.

She laughed and touched his face.

The acoustics of the song continued to force goose bumps onto her skin. Finally, she turned the corner, Harry clutching her arm and saw Phil waiting at the end of the long red mat.

He turned to her, his smile a hundred watts. There had never been a day since she'd known him that he had looked happier.

Kate smiled back. All her doubts, the little voices that nagged in the deep dark night were now silenced. She stepped onto the podium, brushed Phil's hand and allowed a moment of silence to wash over them. Then, she took a deep breath and prepared herself for the brand-new life they were about to begin.

Printed in Great Britain
by Amazon

33381461R00155